me,
you

ALSO BY ERRI DE LUCA

The Day Before Happiness
Three Horses

me,
you

erri de luca

Translated from the Italian
by Beth Archer Brombert

Other Press

NEW YORK

Other Press edition 2011

Copyright © 1998 by Erri De Luca

Translation copyright © 1999 by The Ecco Press

Originally published in Italian as *Tu, Mio* by Giangiacomo Feltrinelli
Editore Milano
Prima edizione ne "I Narrattori" February 1998
Originally published in English as *Sea of Memory* by The Ecco Press

Production Editor: *Yvonne E. Cárdenas*

Text Designer: *Cassandra J. Pappas*

This book was set in 11.5 pt Janson by Alpha Design & Composition
of Pittsfield, NH.

10 9 8 7 6 5 4 3 2 1

Library of Congress Cataloging-in-Publication Data
De Luca, Erri, 1950–
  [Tu, mio. English]
  Me, you = Tu, mio / by Erri De Luca ; translated by Beth Archer
Brombert.
    p. cm.
  Originally published in Italian as Tu, mio; published in English in
1999 under the title: Sea of memory.
   ISBN 978-1-59051-479-5 (pbk.) — ISBN 978-1-59051-480-1
(e-book)
  1. Teenage boys—Fiction. 2. Jewish girls—Fiction. 3. Islands—
Italy—Fiction. 4. World War, 1939–1945—Italy—Fiction.
I. Brombert, Beth Archer. II. Title.
  PQ4864.E5498T813 2011
  853'.914—dc22

                        2011013295

PUBLISHER'S NOTE:
This is a work of fiction. Names, characters, places, and incidents either are the product of the author's imagination or are used fictitiously,
and any resemblance to actual persons, living or dead, events, or lo-
cales is entirely coincidental.

me,
you

A FISH IS a catch once it's in the boat. It's a mistake to shout that you've hooked it when it has only snapped at the bait and you feel its weight bouncing in the hand that holds the line. A fish is a catch only when it's on board. You have to pull it up swiftly from the depths with a gentle, even movement, and without jerking. Otherwise you'll lose it. You mustn't get excited when you feel it thrashing below and it seems heaven only knows how big judging by the force it exerts to extricate the hook and bait from its body.

Nicola taught me how to fish. The boat wasn't his, it was Uncle's, my uncle. Nicola used it year-round, but when the weather was mild he was my uncle's sailor on Sundays and during summer holidays. At night he went out with a lantern and fished for cuttlefish, a kind of squid, to make bait for the tip of the hook.

He got the boat ready and we would leave early in the morning. The island was silent. Going down to the beach barefoot, a boy could feel that he was slippery smooth because of the rock under his feet, that he smelled good because of the fragrance of baking bread that wafted by his nose from the ovens, that he was grown up because he was going out to sea to acquire a skill. The other boys went to the beach later on to meet girls and swim. The rich ones rode around in circles in their motorboats with gleaming wood and multi-horsepowered motors.

Uncle's boat had a lazy diesel that crackled on the calm of dawn and made the air vibrate all around, making my nose itch for the duration of the trip. We would sit on the rail sticking out a bit over the edge, even when the waves came up and pounded the prow. Nicola stood in the stern and maneuvered the handle of the rudder with his feet. It was his trade, he was steady, no wave knocked him off balance. Anyone who could stand upright in a small boat that ran against the waves was steady. I was too, and sometimes on the return trip they let me take the rudder while Uncle slept and Nicola straightened up the boat or cleaned the fish.

It wasn't right for a kid to hold the rudder. You had to go for the other side of the wave and let it pass under the keel without allowing it to strike the boat, because the boat feels the slaps and the wood wears down. But when the sea was calm and there were no boats in sight, I would ask to take the rudder and Nicola could quickly finish what he had left to do.

He taught me the sea thanks to the boat and to the permission of Uncle, who invited me to come along because I kept quiet, I didn't get the line entangled, I didn't budge when the fish bit, didn't complain about the heat, didn't dive off the boat, except for a quick dip to cool off. Never asked to take fish home; it was his fish, and after him, Nicola's. Never asked him to take me with him, but the evening before, it was he who would say, "Come."

Nicola taught me the sea without saying, do it this way. That was the way he did it, and that way was right, not only skillful, but great to watch, never rushed. Nicola's way had the movement of the waves, his gestures had a purpose that I was learning to understand. He would cut the cuttlefish into finger-length pieces, a slice and a stroke with the flat of the blade to separate them, going at an even rhythm of his own, wholly absorbed in his work. The cut pieces dried in the sun during the ride out to open water. He would pierce the bait in the middle, covering the hook all the way up to where the line was attached. And after the catch, he would retrieve the bait from the mouth of the fish, from its throat, and use it over again. Almost without his watching, his hands worked by themselves. He could look elsewhere, far off or nowhere, letting his hands do the work all by themselves. That was the working part, the front of his body, while the rest of it was just an armature of patience.

In the boat only the men talked. I listened to their voices, not to their conversation, and to the greetings exchanged with other fishermen: *"a' re nuost,"* you're one of us, a cry I have only heard at sea.

ℓℓℓ

Some afternoons I went to the fishermen's beach and if I found Nicola alone cleaning fish I would go up to him. Amid the debris of the catch, a hen would scratch around in search of an anchovy head to swallow along with the sand. I was a city boy, but in the summer I turned into a savage. Barefoot, the soles of my feet as leathery as the carobs we ate from the tree, bathing in seawater, salty as a herring, dressed in blue jeans, smelling of fish, a few fish scales in my hair, walking with the short strides of a sailor's gait. In one week I lost my city look. I peeled it off along with the dead skin of my nose and back, where the sun penetrated all the way to the flesh.

The sun is a smoother of surfaces, a kind of sandpaper that during the summer smooths down the earth, evens it out, polishes it, leaving it thin and dry, a film of dust. With the body it does the same thing. Mine, exposed until sundown, split open like a ripe fig, but only in a few places, on my shoulders and nose. I never used sun oil, already available by the mid-fifties. That kind of greasing was for foreigners, shiny skin like a sardine dipped in beaten egg before being fried.

> *Piscitello addevantasse*
> *int'o sciore m'avutasse*
> *m'afferasse sta manella*
> *me menasse int'a tiella*
> *'onn Amalia 'a Speranzella.**

With these lines by Salvatore Di Giacomo, Uncle would make fun of people who oiled themselves.

---

*A little fish I'd become / dusted with flour she'd turn me over / her little hand would grab hold of me / she'd throw me into the pan / donna Amalia Speranzella. (Translator's note, as are all that follow.)

His sons and I, the males of the family, from the time we were little, were used to getting burned at the beginning of the season, and then it stopped. I endured the pain as a perfectly legitimate tax on my delicate city dweller's skin. The new skin cost plenty, on my feet as well before I could walk barefoot on the scorching noonday pebbles.

Nicola had been in the war, an infantryman in Yugoslavia. That had been his only trip, from the island to Sarajevo. He met a family out there. In the evening when he had a pass, he went to visit them, bringing them a little pasta, coffee, bread. They in exchange offered him *slivovitz*, an infernal alcohol that he barely tasted. They communicated in sign language. The Italian Black Shirts had shot one of the sons of that family. It was on that occasion that they got to know each other, when the family came to collect the body. Nicola had helped them and they invited him to their home. He saw a Muslim cemetery: "Like one of ours, but on the stone instead of a cross there was a crescent." He felt at home hearing the sounds of mourning, the same high notes as the wail of the women on his island when the tide brought in a drowning victim. That's how those women sounded with the boy, shot because he was a *partizan*.

He used to tell me these things with the warning that I was not to talk about them with anyone else, that he knew nothing about politics, that these were only stories about when he was young and the war was going on. There was war just as there was the southwester, drought, a season when tuna didn't run. *There was*: a single verb covered all the good and evil that befell human beings. The war lived on in a few odd details that he would relate over and over again: an empty window seen from the street, and behind the window no house, not even a roof, and you could see the sky. Windows are made to see the sky, but not like that. And there was a market square where grass grew because there was nothing to sell and no one ever went there, not even to exchange a few words. Grass can be a sad thing when it grows between the cobblestones of a market.

&c&c&c

He told me a few things because I kept insisting and because that summer he began to trust the boy who copied his gestures, who came to listen to his stories without opening his mouth, without asking this or that. I never repeated his stories, nor did I ever say where I spent some of my afternoons while the other city boys vacationing on the island got together with their first girlfriends. My family didn't ask me to account for my whereabouts, since it was customary for the discipline of the city to be relaxed on the island, except for the observance of mealtimes.

The heat unbound the body. Freedom was a change of skin accompanied by the song of cicadas. The beach was the boundary where the life of men began, a flat surface for those who saw it from the shore, but which was really full of paths, currents, crossroads, depths made shallower by shoals. The boats were keels of perils and miracles; some of them had an olive branch, blessed at Eastertime, tied to a pole in the bow for luck.

I had no personal contact with deep water, nor with those who go deep down with guns. Nicola didn't know how to swim and taught me respect for the depths of the sea. You get from the sea what it gives, not what you want. Our nets, lines, traps, are a request. The reply does not depend on us, on fishermen. Whoever goes below to take the reply with his own two hands lacks respect for the sea. We have a right only to the surface; what lies below is the sea's, is its life. We knock at the entrance, at the surface of the water; we must not enter as though we were masters of the house.

No fishermen armed with guns or oxygen were allowed on Uncle's boat. Uncle saw eye to eye with Nicola. What he liked was the struggle with a grouper that burrows into its hole with a hook in its body, and you need all the power of the boat and the oars to force it out, easing it along the lay of the hole, exhausting its strength to resist. And many a time the grouper would win. By evening hands were raw from the ropes of the suspended fishing tackle that we call *coffa*, and sea salt was encrusted in the cuts and scrapes. These stigmata were renewed at the beginning of each season. Nicola taught me how to harden my palms with a piece of rope.

ᗏᗏᗏ

As a child I heard about the war. At home there were stories told at the table about planes swollen with bombs, sirens that gave little margin of warning, silent races to a shelter, loud growls in the sky followed by the louder growls of explosions on the ground. And once in July with no warning at all bombs fell at random from high up, tearing clumps of the living out of the world in broad daylight. Mama knew these stories: Papa was a soldier. She used to describe their races to the shelters. They fled from the house, a hundred times in their young life, burrowing into the Piedigrotta tunnel in a recurring contest with the other families. Whoever got there first had the best place. Each of us was expected to grab whatever we could and carry it to safety. Mama carried me, Grandpa snatched a suitcase kept near the door in which a set of china tried to stay intact. The women put their valuable things into a handbag that never left their arm in the shelter. Mama remembered a very poor family. The wife always kept an old handbag clutched to her chest. Her children were amazed that she had anything worth saving. One day as she was running to the shelter she fell and her treasure tumbled out: buttons. So as not to lose face, she too had provided herself with an inseparable handbag, stuffing it with buttons to make it look full. Even as bombs fell, a poor woman did not want to look inferior to the others. After that no one ever saw her again.

And after the hundred batterings, the city shook the Germans off its back like a kicking mule, with the kind of kicks that restore dignity to a people. When the Americans did not enter the city, a rebellion suddenly erupted against the Germans and the entire population formed a noose around them, turning their retreat into a rout. Finally the Americans arrived and every family adopted one. In our house there was Jim, a giant of a black man, always cheerful and hardworking. And it was Jim who saved us. After the hundred Allied bombings, a German one arrived. At the wail of the sirens no one wanted to move, it had to be a mistake, the war was over. Jim was in the house and would hear no nonsense. "No, no!" he shouted in his booming voice, forcing everyone out of the house and plucking Mama's grandmother out of her wheelchair, while she screamed for help as she was being carried off by the colossus. And so it was that a German bomb fell smack on the building and on the family's few possessions, evening the score with my father's previously razed house. Mama, who always looked for the funny side when telling these stories, did not forget to add that by the time they reached the shelter, doubled up with laughter over Grandma Emilia's shrieks in Jim's arms, the German bombs were already exploding. She was still laughing about those bombs that had ruined her.

eee

Stories about survival in the city, about interrupted nights, babies who didn't cry, soldiers who escaped

unhurt, German orders plastered everywhere—
these ancient tales were part of childhood. But as I
grew, the time span got shorter. Those events were
no longer remote but recent. That past had barely
taken place; the holes in the streets were still gap-
ing. And when my folks stopped talking about it I
began to ask, which they did not like. My questions
must have had an insistence that I can't remember,
since they sent me to the library in their exaspera-
tion: that's where history is, it's all written down
there, read about it all you like but leave us alone,
we don't want to revive those painful memories.
Things were getting better, they talked about a new
house, our own, not a rental anymore.

The war no longer entered into their stories
around the table, where children became adults as
a result of listening. Instead, they talked about politics, about mayors as piratic as Captain Hook. These
were just pathetic news items, lacking the dimen-
sions of adventure or satire.

That was how I learned their history, a very different subject from the one taught in school out of
textbooks, which explained the past and made it
logical—a free fall all the way down to us. Theirs
was a history filled with infamous events, raids

rather than battles, mass executions, vileness, massacres of defenseless people. It was a history that went nowhere, prepared no sequel, but aspired to be the last, the end of history. Jews—I learned the word from books about the war. Before, they were an ancient people like the Phoenicians, the Egyptians. Jews, but why children, women, old people, hunted in the most wretched places throughout Europe? Strange to learn geography by looking for the cities and regions of the dead: Volhynia, Bukovina, Podolia, Lithuania, a cemetery of flatlands had opened up in the middle of Europe and a boy from Naples looked for it amid the nations awarded to the Soviet Union.

My family stopped asking me what I was reading so as not to have to collide with my determination to know. The questions had multiplied and insidiously held them accountable. Had they taken part in the resistance, had they helped any of the persecuted? No, they hadn't. My mother, still a girl then, had to save her family, and Papa, impoverished by the bombs, flung himself into surviving. He was nonetheless burdened by regret, not to have committed a single act of sabotage, not to have saved anyone outside of himself and his family. He was also burdened by a son who wanted answers. He no longer wanted to discuss the subject with me, so as not to jeopardize his rightful authority. He was sorry to reject my questions but they were becoming more pressing and he had to ward off any suspicion of impertinence: "How dare you speak to your father like that!" I don't remember what "like that" was, but it must have been disrespectful.

Nicola was the only one who talked to me about the war. I would ask, and before answering me he would react to my insistence, "*Si, capòtico.*" It's true, I was stubborn, but only about that. He would reknot the nylon line around a hook, coiling the long length of tackle without looking at me. While he spoke, his breathing came in time to the movement of his hands. He would hold on to part of the line while pulling open a knot with his teeth and the topic might be a snowy night guarding the ammunition dump, or else he might talk about a German reprisal against unarmed people while he swiftly stitched a torn net, his tone remaining flat as he related the story. History had become nothing but an accompaniment to work. Behind us was the island, in front were the afternoon ripples as the *maestrale*, the north wind, subsided. That was the present, most powerful of all, master of time, and Nicola's voice yielded to the place and to the task at hand.

That Sarajevo family saved him after the armistice of the eighth of September* when the Germans imprisoned Italian soldiers in order to send them to work camps in Germany. The family took Nicola into their house and hid him, and when Tito took over they helped him return home.

I was the only person interested in those stories. After the war, the survivors hardened their silence, a callus on the dead skin of wartime. They wanted to live in a new world. Now, Germans were just people who came to the island for vacations. Nicola had nothing to do with them. Hotels and pensioni were far away from the fishermen's beach, which gave off an unending stench of fish guts rotting in the sun. Nicola didn't have to meet Germans, and he didn't want to. He had known them; he didn't want to hear that language with its guttural consonants.

The island was full of Germans, old, middleaged—people who had been young during the war and now in their prosperity hid their former arrogance behind a fake joviality and the pretense of

*On September 8, 1943, the Italian government surrendered to the Allies, but until Germany's defeat in April 1945, those parts of Italy not yet conquered by the Allies were subjected to German occupation. Italian soldiers, formerly German allies, were now prisoners of war; racial laws, largely flouted under fascism, were rigorously observed by the German occupiers.

being merely tourists, never anything else. In organized tour groups and small bands they roamed the island from June to October, apopleptic from the sun, constipated from the lemonades, shiny from their sun oils like the baba au rhum at the Bar Calise.

They were the same ones. Nicola watched them from afar and when one of them asked for directions he replied with the only words he had learned: *ich verstehe nicht*, I don't understand. He had seen them in Yugoslavia and no longer wanted to understand them. The islanders, on the other hand, spoke whatever little German was necessary for business.

Nicola stood with his back to the island and saw only those few who came across the short stretch of beach that lay between his feet and the sea.

I didn't like the Germans either. They were the same ones I had found in the books about that infamous period, the ones who had let themselves be intoxicated and ruined by Hitler, and no defeat had been able to strip them of their arrogant madness. The defeated ones were the others, the ones who served them during their vacations on a southern island.

Where my aversion grew abstractly out of books, Nicola's was made of flesh. Incapable of hostility, he reacted with outbursts of timidity. One day he told me that the year before, he had recognized a German soldier, one who had been in Sarajevo. They looked at each other, neither one spoke. But Nicola felt the teeth of war tear at his gut. He turned red with shame. He had been in church at the time, at Mass. He left without even crossing himself: *"Me so' mmiso scuorno pe'Ddio,"* he was ashamed for God. *"Adda tene' pacienza pure int'a casa soia,"* one had to have patience even in one's own house. The word *pacienza* is particularly nice in Neapolitan because it contains the word *pace*, peace, within patience. I asked him if he had ever killed anyone. No reply. He was teaching me not to expect a reply to all my questions.

When Nicola ran into them on the island, he crossed to the other side of the street. I knew stories about the Warsaw ghetto where the Germans prohibited the Jews from looking them in the eye. That summer I started to stare at them, not as a challenge but in an effort to understand. It was rare for any of them to notice.

❧❧❧

It was the summer of my sixteenth year, my emotions were on edge. Unlike my coevals, I was not attracted to girls of my own age. I liked older ones, an impossible desire. That summer, however, I did get my wish. I was the only one of my contemporaries to spend time with them.

That was thanks to Daniele, my uncle's son, who was four years older than I. He was the head of a group of young men of good family who had scooters, and a few of them had boats. Though without such means himself, Daniele was nonetheless the born leader of any group. He was a guest in the house my parents rented, and slept in the same room with me. That summer he became aware of me. I can't account for his interest, but that's how it was. He taught me chords on the guitar, he took me to the place on the beach where his friends got together and let me stay with them. My skinny looks, intensified by my sudden growth, were not much to talk about—fuzz on my cheeks more yellow than blond, narrow eyes, a tight jaw that never relaxed. Perhaps he saw me as more mature or sensed that in his cousin an avalanche was gathering.

I did not go on their excursions to distant places on the island and rarely joined their evening get-togethers or the dances they held spontaneously wherever they went. But I did join them at the beach when I came back from fishing. Over the previous few years Daniele had begun staying out late and was little inclined to get up early. He stopped going out with his father and Nicola. I took his place. And so when I came back from fishing, I would go find him and he would ask me to tell him all about our day's expedition.

ᕲᕲᕲ

That summer I had a baptism of blood caused by a moray eel. It was pulled up on the same line with a grouper. While Uncle and Nicola were busy with the fish, I tried to detach the hook from the moray's throat. I squeezed its cheeks with my left hand to keep its mouth open. Just as I was getting the hook out, the moray wriggled. I lost my grip on its jaws and its teeth sank into my hand at the joint of the index finger. A moray doesn't just bite; where it grabs hold it doesn't let go. Once it sets its jaw, it doesn't open it again. I managed not to scream, but tears welled in my eyes from the effort. When he finished with the grouper and Uncle resumed pulling up the line, Nicola noticed me and with one stroke of his knife beheaded the moray. Then he broke the jawbone, and only then took the teeth out of my hand, one by one. I kept looking at the sea

while Nicola performed this ancient little opera-
tion, my wounded hand far from my thoughts. Pain
was knocking but I wouldn't open up. I had heard
tales about what happened to me. I had previously
experienced the venom of a weever in the sole of
my foot and that of a scorpion fish in my palm. I was
in a fishing boat and that was part of the deal. Uncle
gave me a half smile between one armful of line and
another, nodding his head. *"Mo' si' pescatore,"* now
you're a fisherman, Nicola said, when he finished
rinsing my hand in seawater.

I didn't really understand why masculinity meant
having to ignore pain. I saw it exercised by men and
tried to do the same when it came my turn. I understood that it was not a rejection of the body but the
patience to endure it, a load on a beast of burden
that is too heavy at times and can even kill, but up
to that point you don't complain. The body was a
patient beast that men tamed with pride. The body
was ruled by the unyielding codes of southern virility. The spines of the sea urchin that boys learned to
pull out by themselves were left in by fishermen to
be slowly absorbed beneath the skin. I was learning
from them how to detach oneself from pain.

When I reached the beach I was feverish from the
effort of controlling myself. A vein in my forehead

was throbbing. Daniele asked me to tell him what had happened and showed off the glory of my wound to everybody. That gesture of his which made me seem important, that kindness, relieved the pain in my eyes. The curiosity of a girl I had never seen before, the contact of her hands with my multi-punctured one, relieved the pain there too. What remained was a swollen vein that pounded in my temple.

I looked squarely at that new girl and she broke into an open laugh, ringing like coins falling out of a piggy bank when it breaks. Her teeth, one slightly nicked in the middle of her mouth, shimmered white between her full lips, and her hair cascaded over half her face. My heart lurched. Then the demonstration of the wound ended and I heard Daniele speak the name of the new girl. Her name was Caia.

A strange name, the feminine of Caio,* and even her voice was strange, a bit nasal but clear, with a foreign accent layered on soft Italian—a pleasing lightness in the midst of the heavy cadence of the south. She had just arrived, a guest of one of the girls in the group, with whom she roomed in a Swiss boarding school. She was Rumanian. She had no

---

*Even in the masculine it is rare as a name but is widely used in the expression, Tizio, Caio, Sempronio, the equivalent of Tom, Dick, or Harry.

family. Daniele told me about her then and there but he didn't know much. She answered the boys' queries with an absent smile, dismissing them with a shrug of her shoulders that was a fraction of a dive, like a body that pushes off from the rocks and swims way out. It wasn't necessary to know more about her. For the boys, her orphan's freedom was enough of an attraction. None of them knew what it was to be alone in the world.

No one understood what caught her fancy: it wasn't the luxurious things owned by rich people— not even the extravagance of a motorboat that one of them had at his disposal.

eee

Because of Daniele I was admitted to the group, but as an outsider. The girls didn't come near me, not even for helpful services, those minimal opportunities for chivalry. I liked to be with them nevertheless, but even more when Caia was there.

"Your name is Katia?" I asked, thinking her name might be Slavic.

"No, Caia," she replied brusquely, turning away. I had taken the chance of approaching her and was rejected, things that happened in a small group all enmeshed in miniature hierarchies. I took it badly, not imagining that she could behave like the other girls. And why not? I defensively convinced myself that she was just like the others. A beautiful, well-bred girl allows herself to be approached only by those she likes. It was a logical explanation, but it didn't satisfy me. Had I been mistaken? What on earth could have made me think her name was Katia? Hadn't I heard her called Caia more than once? What was I seeking: to divine, to unearth something the others had overlooked? I think so. That was the motive behind my question, her name. I started from there, from the accident that stays with the life of a person more closely than a shadow, because at least in the dark a shadow lets go, but not a name. And it wants to be so much a part of that person that it presumes to explain that person, to announce the person: "I am," then the name follows, as though one can *be* a name rather than *have* a name. I realized later that she hadn't said, "I am Caia," but, "My name is Caia."

She was not Caia, a name, she was a person who had that name. Maybe she wanted to keep that little bit of identity to herself, or maybe she didn't like it. There, I was already investigating her, in search of something she held private. That's how you fall in love, looking for the one thing in the person you love that hasn't been revealed to anyone else, that is given as a gift only to the one who searches and listens with love. You fall in love when you're nearby, but not too near. You fall in love from a corner of a room, off to the side, near a table full of people, on a terrace where the others are dancing to the heavy beat of some silly pop song that plasters a face to your heart like a poster. From the first moment, I fell hopelessly in love with Caia, an older girl, with a chipped tooth in a blinding smile, who had touched my hand without revulsion for the wound and who had become close to me because of it. I fell in love out of an impulse that ran counter to the facts: that I was much more mature, that it was my duty to protect her from the perils of the island, to guard her secret which I didn't yet know but which had to exist and which I would learn, I alone.

ᕮᕮᕮ

When she impulsively ran from the beach umbrella to the sea without alerting anyone, I didn't follow her, which would have made me look ridiculous, but I followed her every stroke as intently as a chained watchdog. If there were high waves my breath became audible, a gargle, a snarl, and if I could no longer restrain myself I walked toward the water with feigned nonchalance in order not to lose sight of her behind a wave. If she dived in with the others, I was at ease. It didn't matter to me if she turned someone's head in the morning and someone else's in the evening. My concern was to protect her. Not one of those boys could get near her secret. Perhaps I couldn't either, but I had gotten it into my head that there was one, that within Caia was a revelation that could be reached with love. I was making no progress with her; I no longer had the nerve to speak to her.

Daniele was the obvious choice for Caia's love. I imagined him singing along with the guitar of an evening. His voice was a touch strained, a little husky, but he could lower it to a whisper without losing the music. His singing surged out of him and when you heard him you began breathing deeply, holding your breath at times. Caia was bound to fall for Daniele, lean, well built; he hooked you with his smile. That was not my business, since I wasn't a candidate for her affection and I certainly wasn't jealous. I never knew whether there was anything between them. If so, it didn't last long. Every one of those boys thought he would be chosen by Caia for at least the evening, and would receive from her arms a sign of preference. She would look at a boy from under her chestnut tresses, eyes wide open, lips slightly parted, hesitating a moment before a word fell out: that was as far as the invitation went. For her those boys were still puppies, great bodies, but clumsy with words. Then again, it was summer; you can't be too demanding of casual encounters.

ᴇᴇᴇ

Daniele soon lost interest in Caïa. His pride did not allow for falling in love a little bit, just for one evening. He nevertheless remained affectionate toward her and attentive to her voice amid the babble of the group. He wasn't thinking about secrets, like me, yet he did understand that there was an impenetrable ache in that girl which left for love only the occasional eruption of a smile. Granted, she was an orphan, growing up in a boarding school, and there the knot inside her must have tightened. The girl whose guest she was liked her a lot. They had become acquainted the year she was sent abroad to study languages. Caïa, a veteran of the school, took her under her wing, making it easier for her to get used to a new place and to strangers. They became friends, but not even she knew anything worth mentioning about Caia. She wasn't exactly sad, just moody at times, but basically cheerful.

A crystal glass broke and the gleaming shards scattered all over the floor, breaking into fragments. Caia laughed at the troubled face of the boy who was trying to clean up the mess and her laughter was a perfect echo of those fragments. Because I was studying chemistry, I happened to say, not to her directly but as an aside about her laughter: "Caia has silicon in her vocal chords." And she, turning toward me, said suddenly but quietly, "My father was a chemist." I was so astounded that I didn't make a move in her direction. I stayed put, swallowing hard. No one around us had heard. No one seemed to have taken notice of this surprising event, everybody was otherwise occupied. Her father was a chemist. She had wanted to say it, and spontaneously, more than in response to me. It had slipped out, perhaps unwillingly, but in this one thing something of her pain and her secret came to light, and I had brought it about. I was moved, and felt even more compelled to protect her. Something had happened between us, a secret exchange, an understanding. I was no longer the kid who went fishing, wore the mark of the trade on his hand, and was always mute. What I was besides that I didn't know, couldn't know, but my distance from her had been bridged. Caia had done it with a piece of news communicated to no one else.

At their gatherings around a table I participated from a back row. If they were in a pizzeria I also took a seat but I didn't eat with them, and they didn't invite me to do so. Boys of my age did not go out to dinner. I would meet Daniele and the others after I had eaten at home. I would stay and watch their high spirits, their noisy laughter, and even in the confusion of their voices I could single out Caia's laughter from the others. I would play a stupid game. I'd put an ice cube in my mouth and hold it there until it melted, while the nerves in my mouth turned into a tangle of thorns. My teeth froze and I could feel their roots pulsate. They were the keys of a painful organ. With my eyes shut tight, the clamor disintegrated in my ears and I could isolate Caia's voice, separating it from the noise. The nerves of my mouth jangled for a moment, Caia's timbre resounded in my head, in my frozen teeth which were as sensitive as antennae. I heard her voice with my teeth. Boys go in for tortures in their search for ecstasy. No one paid any attention to me. I could leave without saying goodbye. If I caught Daniele's eye, I could tell him I was leaving with a glance.

Maybe Caia liked grown men. I later heard rumors about her crush on Uncle. He was in his forties, was attractive to women, and knew how to tell them they were attractive to him. Uncle was the opposite of the beach macho. There was a sobriety about him, his gestures were measured, precise, more restrained than those of most southerners. His American mother had endowed his looks with something from the West, from the open plains, in his clear eyes, his smooth forehead, the flash of spurs in his smile. You could hear the gallop in his open-throated laugh. During the summer he wore nothing but a shirt tied at the waist, a pair of unpressed pants, and went barefoot. He had an elegance in his carriage that was inimitable. I watched him walk out of a room, open a door, hold a glass, and couldn't help but recognize that no one could do those things so well. He was always aware of his body. And if he happened to have an accident, ran into a door or stubbed his bare foot, even in his clumsiness he was elegant, dignified, not even then was he awkward. Many years later, when he let himself die rapidly, it was because he had ceased being at the center of his body.

If there had ever been an intimacy, an infatuation between Uncle and Caia, I never even suspected it. Still, I had seen them together at the beach, at friends' houses, and there was a playfulness between them, but in jest, not like when he knew he was raising goose bumps on a woman's body. I did not see him turn on his charm with Caia, not in his voice nor in those attentive gestures that made a woman queen for an hour.

I noticed nothing, not even the time Caia came with Daniele and went fishing with us. It had been decided at the last moment, which was why I found myself on the beach early one morning, one person too many. Uncle looked annoyed. Daniele had not told me to stay home. I made my excuses to Uncle and said good-bye to them all. But Caia broke in with a peremptory outburst that was inappropriate. Her sudden interference took us by surprise because a woman, a girl, had no right barging into men's affairs. "He is here and he comes with us!"— said in a tone it was better to pretend not to have heard. Light was breaking, the sea was calm, her words made a small commotion. Uncle looked at her squarely, beckoned with his head, and I pushed off, jumping into the boat as it slid into the water. Caia's mood instantly brightened when she saw she had prevailed. Uncle gave her a quick smile in return.

If you go out in a small fishing boat with lines, you can't drop too many, since they easily get tangled on the bottom because of currents and fish snapping at them, and then it's a job to get them untangled. I knew that, and for that reason I didn't fish that day, but I didn't care. I did mind, however, that Uncle had an extra person on board. With five people it's crowded, so that on the way out, I sat in the bow with my legs over the rail to keep out of the way. Nicola was at the rudder, Uncle was stretched out, Daniele was cutting bait. Caia came forward. She lay down with her head near my knee. I could look down at her, at a strand of her hair that fell over the rail and bounced with the rocking of the boat. The sea shimmered so brightly behind her I had to squint.

"At times you have certain gestures that remind me of someone who loved me." She spoke softly, below the level of noise from the diesel motor. I blushed as though she had shouted this to the entire world from a loudspeaker. She had spoken without opening her eyes.

"And you felt the same way about him?"

Caia gave a little nod.

We headed for the shoals of Capri. The trip took a long time; the noise of the motor helped her to talk. I tuned my ear to the frequency of her voice, which I could have made out in a gale. From the stern you couldn't tell that we were talking. I replied without looking at her, staring straight ahead, speaking words into the wind. I saw a wave rise up higher than the others and understood it would make her head bump against the wood. And so at the moment the bow made contact, I slid my hand between her neck and the boat to cushion the blow. I then withdrew it at once. Caia looked at me from underneath, her face serious, like a child at a window waiting for someone to return. She was seeing something far away, behind me, a hand that had held her head who knows how long ago. I kept my eyes fixed on her. She seemed to be seeing me against the sky without anyone around, without land.

I think we were talking about religion. She had one; she liked to invoke a remote *You,* but not in a church or in any enclosed place. I replied that I knew nothing about God or love. She believed that there were spirits capable of staying with us and never abandoning us. I, on the other hand, had no one I could call a spirit or an angel, and no notion of what she was feeling. She said that sometimes spirits feel the need to make themselves known, and so for a few seconds enter into the body of someone nearby and through it make some gesture or say something by which she can recognize their presence. But it happens so fast she doesn't have enough time to communicate that she has received their signal. Did that ever happen to me? Never. No, even if I wanted to say: I too, always, like you, anywhere, yes, from now on I will recognize those I don't even know. But I couldn't lie to Caia, not even to please her in her first attempt to speak to me under the cover of a diesel motor.

Daniele called her and she went back to the stern to learn how to put bait on a hook. When the boat was over the shoals and the motor was turned off, voices reached me in the bow, wavering, fragmented, as though from a pail at the bottom of a well. I dropped the anchor, secured it, and came to the middle of the boat as Daniele lowered his line from the bow. Uncle was in the stern, Nicola and Caia on either side, and for as long as it took for the weights to reach the bottom, there was a rapid whoosh of nylon against the palm of the hand. Caia had the first nibble, a shock that frightened a shriek out of her. Uncle instantly

heard the line bounce. Dashing to his feet, he gestured with his arm to pull up. Then Nicola had one,
then Daniele; we were over a whole school. So as not
to pull up all the lines at once, Nicola told me to hold
his while he kept Caia from tangling the line that
was being pulled into the boat. I could feel the fish
on Nicola's hooks, at least two. I pulled the line up a
few meters to raise their wriggling out of the middle
of the school so that the other fish wouldn't be frightened away. "*Nzerréa,*" Nicola said about the first line
brought up. The weight of the hooked fish made the
nylon line rubbing along the edge of the boat produce a cicadalike sound, "nzrr, nzrr," as each arm's
length came up. "*Nzerréa,*" Nicola said, and Daniele
repeated the verb to Caia, explaining its meaning.
The plump, shiny fish, shimmering white against the
black depths of the sea, were brought on board.

"*Ianchéa,*" Nicola said of his catch, it's all white.

"*Ianchéa,*" Uncle said of his own.

Daniele, however, pulled up a furious red scorpion fish, its spines rigid, especially the second one,
the poisonous dorsal spine that required great care
when grabbing the fish to remove the hook. Daniele
was quick, he had not forgotten how to do it. He had
learned from Nicola, better than I. Nicola. The name
of the island's patron saint, one in every family, a

name given to boats and churches, and even to the mountain that pokes through the grove of chestnut trees. Nicola. He went back to the line he had entrusted to me. I told him quietly that I had pulled it up a few arm's lengths and he nodded in approval.

※※※

It was a good catch. The wooden basin was packed with fish. Caia had fun counting how much each of us had caught. As was bound to happen, she got her line all tangled. She had pulled it on board in a hurry, letting it drop at her feet. When she tried to lower it again, it had turned into a bird's nest of nylon. I set myself to untangling it, sitting at her feet on the plank floor. "You look as if you're sewing," she said about the way I raised my arm high to unravel the ball, giving it enough slack to loosen itself. It took me a quarter of an hour, pretty good for that kind of mess. Uncle explained to her that she should let the line fall between her feet without stepping on it. He was no longer annoyed about being crowded. The day was serene, there were no other boats around. The coast of the island drifted away behind the mist.

We were far out, no land in sight, no shade on the boat. It must have been noon. The current alone kept the bow aligned with the anchor and slapped at the stern, placing it slightly southeast. There was barely a breath of the *maestrale*, the north wind.

Uncle dived into the water, followed by Caia and Daniele. Nicola and I held the lines. I splashed some water on my head but did not go in for a swim. Nicola said not a word to Caia. Women fishing? He wouldn't dream of taking them; it wasn't done. Not that they were in the way, but he felt intimidated. "Makes me uncomfortable," he would say.

On the return trip Daniele took the rudder, Uncle lowered a trolling line from the stern, Nicola set to work cleaning the fish. I went forward and Caia joined me.

"If a big wave comes, protect my head."

I would have given blood for some rough water, but we were moving with the current, the waves pushing us ahead, and Daniele was good at taking advantage of the right angle for sliding down the crest of the waves as though going downhill. There was no chance for me to cushion her neck. Caia fell asleep. I would have liked to wet her hair so that her head didn't get too hot, but I was afraid to wake her. I managed to place myself so that at least I shaded her head with my body. She slept with her lips parted. I would have liked to put my ear near her breath and listen to it. There was more than breath in that sleep; there must have been words as well, perhaps in a language I wouldn't have understood. I would have liked to put my nose into that breath and sniff it as it came up from the depth of her chest, becoming perfumed in her throat, its fragrance mingling with the incense of her saliva. I would have smelled the red gills of her river fish, the mist of Swiss forests. I would not have wanted to put my mouth on her breath. My mouth would have understood nothing she exhaled, my mouth would only have sucked recklessly, brazenly stealing the air of her breathing. My body, cramped from the way I was sitting, shaded her, fulfilling its function of guardian.

There is no return, I thought, this trip lacks symmetry, it only goes one way.

If Caia had been involved with both Uncle and Daniele, on that day's fishing trip she managed to find a mid-point between the two of them, but only when she was in the bow. On awaking she laughed at the fishy smell on her hands. Only later did I learn that her insistence on my coming along that morning was the counterbalance of another trip when she had been prevented from taking with her someone who remained behind.

ᘒᘒᘒ

Our summers on the island lasted for months. We were there long enough to want to stay forever. Leaving the island felt like going into exile. One year there was an outbreak of polio in the city and so we remained on the island until November. Without the summer the island was an empty shell: unheated rooms, silent cicadas in the pine groves. I was a child then and I thought of the island as a shield. Evil came from the land and had to surrender in the face of the sea.

Daniele composed songs, some of them quite nice, certainly nicer than the ones on records. That summer I had a guitar. He would borrow it for the evening, but even in our room he would play something. He thought up music for the prayers of Our Father and Holy Mary. The melodies turned out very well; he sang them to me softly without the words. I didn't know how to pray; I didn't even know how to ask people for help.

ᘒᘒᘒ

It's a good thing that stories in books are soundless, otherwise I would try to sing those songs right here, within these pages. They moved you deep down, without being solemn, or needing an organ, at most a violin. That's how he was, but he could also be hard, even aloof at times. It's that mixture which can produce a natural leader, the kind that speaks up in a crowd and makes everybody follow him. He never did anything like that, but I later knew such men and often realized how much more exceptional and appealing they would have had to be in order to be a Daniele.

The other boys copied his gags, his grimaces, even his walk. I didn't have that gift of mimicry. I willingly obeyed him, learned his songs and his chords, but I couldn't have repeated any of his jokes. They were his; from any other mouth it was ridiculous. Like a mother beaming at her little boy, Caia listened to him sing, smiling encouragingly. One could only rejoice in their affinity.

There was no other occasion to be close to Caia. I kept remembering the things she said in the boat, about my reminding her of someone, without telling me who, nor would I ever ask. I had the nest egg of a confidence that came to me by chance, but I was no closer to her secret. I was still on the surface, waiting for some word to come from her. I was too young to force it out of her and my ineffectiveness made me miserable. There was not a soul I could talk to without betraying myself.

I spent my days fishing in the morning, then back to the beach, a visit with Nicola if he was in front of his house, and in the late afternoon I looked for Daniele's crowd. Days without change. Evenings, I watched the sun go down too fast. With Daniele I never spoke unless he spoke first. He liked Caia, but there were others. She was attractive but not important to him. Had I talked to him about Caia, he would have made fun of me.

One afternoon I asked Nicola if he remembered the girl who had come fishing with us. He nodded his head. To induce him to say something, I invented the story that she was going out with Daniele. Nicola said nothing and continued to arrange the lines of the multi-hook rig. He gave a little sigh and shook his head. Was there something he didn't like about her?

"It's none of my business, but it's better to go with girls of your own kind."

Did he have something against Rumanians? Nicola wasn't concerned about that, that's not what he was talking about. Caia was Rumanian, did he know that? No, he didn't know where Rumania was. He remained silent for a while, his hands falling idle, which made me think I was bothering him. I was about to apologize when he said with effort, "The girl is not one of those people you're talking about."

What the devil could he know about it? Two conflicting emotions made the blood rush to my face: anger and shame. Finally I was able to talk about her, and I was hearing offensive suspicions from someone who had seen her only one morning and had not addressed a word to her. I was about to stand up when Nicola said gruffly, lowering his voice, "The girl is Jewish," stressing the *dj* sound. I looked at him, narrowing my eyes. A chasm opened between us, a collision, a slap, a betrayal. Why? How did he know? But I couldn't bring myself to ask. An anchor had plunged into my throat.

"The name is Jewish. In Sarajevo there were lots of Jewish women whose names were Sara and Caia. Not Caia, the way we say it, with a *k* sound, but with a heavy *h*, like when you clear your throat, Chaie. The little girls were called Chaiele, Sorele. There were lots of them, and then they were taken away. First they were locked up, then they were put on trains, not in coaches, but in freight cars. By the time we arrived, all the men were gone. People said they had all been killed by the Germans. The only ones remaining were women, children, and a few old people."

His hands had remained still, his head bowed over them. Then, before returning to his work, he added in closing, *"Gualgiò, che brutta carogna è 'a guerra,"* Oh kid, what a dirty rotten thing war is.

And what kind of a war was it? A war against women, babies? What kind was your war?

"What do you want to know? When you came along it was all over, no Germans, no Jews, all you saw were Americans, smuggling, black market, a whole business of dollars. I could talk till tomorrow, tell you what the war I saw was like, you'd still know nothing. You have to know with your own eyes, with fear, an empty stomach, not with ears and books. We were twenty years old, they pressed us like olives, and like olives we didn't make a sound. There were Jewish women, they asked us to save their children, they handed them over to us, *to us*, Italian soldiers who were the enemy, and we could do nothing." Nicola choked up on his last words and couldn't go on.

Nothing. Only you, Nicola, managed to say this word, digging it out of helplessness and fear. Nothing. There are nothings that you can never get rid of. Each time I hear someone say "nothing," it rings false; they don't know how to say it. They don't know what nothing is. You know, Nicola, and those women who handed their children over to enemy strangers, they knew. I couldn't reply. I was a kid who didn't even understand sunlight. Caia was a Jew. I was mortified not to have thought of it myself, with all my pretensions at discovering a secret from those crumbs she had confided in me. How was I different from the other city boys vacationing on the island? They were hospitable by nature, by indolent custom, not out of any genuine wish to meet people or get to know them. Caia was just a funny name for us. The accident of fate that sent a fisherman from the south to make war in Yugoslavia provided the most basic fact. She came from a people who had been eliminated house by house, her parents killed. Her life had depended on being saved, unlike ours, exposed at worst to the ills of the south. Perhaps she was one of the children placed in the arms of a stranger who carried her to safety.

I asked Nicola to repeat her name to me, as he remembered it, and its diminutive: Chaie, Chaiele, Chaie, Chaiele: a thick *h* never heard before, followed by the vowels of a little shout. I was learning her secret by pronouncing her name. I was afraid someone might already know about it, but Nicola had told no one, not even Uncle. In fact, he didn't want to talk about it at all, and rightly so because he had let this slip, but only because I had asked him to talk to me about the war. He regretted having told me and asked me not to repeat it to anyone. It wasn't right to put your nose in other people's business. I promised willingly, relieved. I said I had understood nothing, that I could not have figured it out by myself. In his rapid dialect Nicola said: "I don't even understand the sea. Don't know why a boat floats, why wind and storms make waves on the sea and dust on land. I live by the sea because I was born to it, but I don't understand a thing about it. What is it after all? It's just sea, water and salt, but it's deep, very deep."

And then he left me troubled by the thought that perhaps the girl didn't know anything about her own background. In that case, her secret was mine alone. I couldn't even share it with her.

℮℮℮

I got up from the sand of the fishermen's beach reeling, drunk, consumed with shame. Without Nicola, master even of that, I would never have known anything about the most sought-after truth. Caia's secret was handed to me as a gift, in view of the fact that I would never have acquired it all by myself. I wandered off to the Aragonese castle on the bridge of the isthmus that connected it to the land. I climbed down among the rocks in search of a blank space for my eyes, stopping at a point that opened out to the horizon and nothing else, just water. Dusk was falling. Exhausted by my emotional upheaval, I fell asleep. It was night when I woke up, my head was cold, the sky packed with stars. My steps were wooden at first, then looser, and then I broke into a run which set me racing through deserted streets, accompanied from time to time by hunting dogs left loose on the island. Aimless happiness, warm stones under my soles, soft breezes in my ears, my throat parched, I broke into the house like a thief. Daniele was asleep in my room whistling through his nose, my guitar lying on his sandals. I picked it up and hung it on its nail. Its sounding box pinged a delicate A on contact, and in my head the name Chaie, Chaiele kept coming back, telling me why I felt happy. I murmured the name until sleep overtook me.

In the morning I was faced with my mother's reproaches and Daniele's questions. I had fallen asleep on the beach, having gone to watch them fish with lanterns, and had no awareness of sleeping on the warm sand. That half lie came out with cheeky veracity. I never told lies. Daniele said that's what he had thought, and had proposed going to look for me precisely on the beach. It would not happen again, I promised. In our family, oaths were not permitted. It was enough to say with conviction, I promise.

ℰℰℰ

Chaie, Chaiele became music in my ears. I repeated it in the morning, barely awake, I put my thoughts to rest with it at bedtime. Lovers pray with only one word, a name. I didn't write it, I didn't pronounce it out loud; I couldn't jeopardize the secret by leaving traces behind.

One evening I was with Daniele's crowd on a terrace very close to the sea; they were having a party. A boy kept putting on records with a fast beat, dances with a lot of jumping and turning, and Caia bounced back and forth amid arms and shirts, or so I saw her from my observation spot. Needing a rest, she came and sat down next to me, a friendly gesture. I had no idea that she had seen me. She wiped away a film of perspiration with the back of her hand and as a joke spread it on my face. I smiled over the borrowed sweat and didn't wipe it off. The music started up again. She declined to go back, putting off till later the boys who called out to her. Daniele was standing off in a corner with a girl. Caia turned her back to the party and faced the sea so that we sat side by side but in opposite directions.

"At times I see the world upside down," she said. "When I was a child there was a river with trees along the banks. I would turn it around and see the trees holding up the river, the bridges were hammocks for lying down in the shade of the river's current. Even today I see the sky as a floor."

Her voice made no attempt to be heard, it was very low, but she knew I would hear her. Without changing position on the stone ledge, I leaned back, clasping my hands behind my head.

"Dancing looks like a race to me, everybody rushing to get caught." I invented this idea so as not to remain silent after her remarks, to prove that I had heard her, that I would always hear.

"Is that why you don't dance, so as not to be caught?" she shot back with a smile. "I'll catch you now." And she stood up, pulling me by the arm.

I tried to resist. They'd only laugh. I didn't know a single dance step.

"If you can stand up in a boat, you can dance."

I didn't try to argue that it was the contrary, that balance on the sea was a resistance to swaying, to losing one's footing. I said to her in my final entreaty, "Everybody wants to dance with you. If you take a turn with me you'll make them hate me. As it is, it's a lot for them to have a kid hanging around."

"You're not a kid, you're an old man, you're ancient, another generation. I dub you my knight of old."

She pulled so hard I couldn't resist without hurting her. I went to the record player and put on a slow song. She took me by the hand, placing my other one behind her back, and led me into the music. The others took advantage of the record to do the same.

"Why did you say I'm an old man?" I asked her, surprised by the deep timbre that issued from my throat.

"You've suddenly become an old man in a marvelous way. You are someone who has come from far away, like me, someone who has disembarked in a new land, has gray hair, and wonders how he is going to get along."

The bite of the moray had left a pattern of holes: a pale letter on dark skin. Her hand was right on that spot and it was the most intimate gesture I had ever experienced with a woman. She was touching the surface of a pain, in a clasp as capable of reviving it as assuaging it. I'm here, her hand said, holding the wound for the duration of the song. I'll go with you far away and hold your pain in my hand.

I yielded to her willful grasp on the bite, barely swaying, less than on a boat at evening. She held me in her arms, without squeezing, in a light but firm hold. I followed, and inside of me another age took place, remote, beyond time. I became what she saw in me and wanted me to be. Chaie, Chaiele, her name beat in my head to the rhythm of the music, of our feet as they brushed each other in a turn. I could hear the waves crashing against the rocks; her name resounded in the roar. Her breath fell against my wrinkled collar. I was no longer a kid next to her. Chaie, Chaiele was the breath of everything around, as though speaking her name, and I heard it inside my head like a beat to keep me from losing my step: Chaie, Chaiele.

"What did you say?" she asked, stopping abruptly and backing away from me. "What did you say?"

Nothing. I didn't think I said anything.

"No, you said . . . you called me . . . what did you call me?"

I didn't reply. She stood still in front of me, her voice tense with anger, a frightened look in her eyes. I couldn't have said her name, I couldn't. Somebody changed the record, putting on something wild and noisy. Caia pulled me by the arm outside the dance area and said furiously, "Don't you ever call me by that name again, ever!" Her voice broke on each word. I must have been looking at her with stricken eyes, like an innocent victim, like an old man. She pressed her lips together and swallowed hard. "Go get me something to drink. No, never mind, I'll go myself." And she walked away.

I went back to the ledge for a while, then went out to the rocks, heading home. The music grew fainter, at last overwhelmed by the sea, and then I could say out loud my "Chaie, Chaiele." It was my natural voice again, not that shadowy voice that came out of me when I was close to her. My own voice could not have betrayed the secret by speaking her name; it was saying it now, for the first time, at the edge of the sea. Could the touch of her arms have confused me to the point of not knowing whether I was speaking or not? Chaie, Chaiele. Nicola was right, except for the question of awareness: Caia knew who she really was in the midst of others, and who were her intimates.

For a few days I didn't join Daniele or even go fishing much. Uncle had guests on the boat. In the afternoon I stayed longer than usual at Nicola's, hearing about the trip and what they caught. It was the time of Uncle's vacation and Nicola went out every night to drop the baited lines. He would return home and sleep a few hours before meeting Uncle on the beach and going out with him to bring in the lines. They caught an occasional grouper, more often congers and morays, a few scorpion fish, starfish, even gulls, who followed the boats despite the darkness and dived at the lines, getting caught on the hooks and dragged to the bottom. Once we caught a sea turtle but Uncle put it back after an exchange of knowing glances with Nicola. We saw it swim toward the bottom with leisurely strokes, not at all in frantic flight.

September was nice, when you go trolling for tuna, sea urchins, needlefish, and there isn't all that work needed for multi-hook rigs. I stood beside Nicola and did the easiest part, which was to arrange the hooks by attaching them to the edge of the cork while he fed me the line and then coiled it into a basket. And we got around to talking, picking up where we had left off the last time. All around us the other fishermen were doing the same thing helped by young boys. Nicola's sons were still too little. The village houses stood on the shore facing the beached boats. The fishermen helped each other pull in a boat or drag it into the water without having to ask.

The air was filled with the shouts of children and the stench of bilgewater mixed with a powerful smell of tar and a touch of diesel fuel that leaked from the motors. A fisherman's life was not purely natural, but combined the crafts of a carpenter, a mechanic, a tailor, and only in deep water, at the very end of his work, came the fish and the tools for catching them.

There was always something to be done and dusk fell as we stood side by side, facing the sea, while the light dimmed to darkness between our hands. The fishing village caught the last rays. I told him he was right, that he had known the Germans and I the Americans, he the war and I the slow discovery of having been born in a city that had sold itself. The Americans were the bosses, not the criminal tyrants he had known, just the bosses. The mayor was their spokesman, the port was their dock, the bay was crawling with fleets of their ships, aircraft carriers, submarines, cruisers, and the city was the playground for thousands of foreign sailors and soldiers, the masters of the field. The city was the largest bordello in the Mediterranean. They urinated all over the place, which I saw as their mark on our territory.

Our police were powerless during the landings. They had their own police, their own neighborhoods, their own stores, vehicles, movies. Nicola listened without understanding the shame I felt at having that American in my home. They were there because they had liberated us, but in Naples they never finished with their liberation. In the rest of Italy no other cities were held by the Americans, but Naples had become the wartime capital of the southern Mediterranean. They were in command and we were just one of many military ports of call, held on to for strategic reasons. That year I suddenly felt ashamed for my sold-out city.

"Do you hate the Americans?"

No, Nicola, they're just doing their job, sniffing a little at the stink of us Latins. They run around looking blank or else suspicious, and if you see any other expression in their faces it comes from alcohol. I hate the Germans without ever having seen them in uniform, as you did, and I hate the officials who govern my city which they presented with thighs wide open to the sailors. Nicola admitted to having hated the Germans, but not anymore.

"Today they're just tourists, even if I can't stand that language of theirs. I seem to hear again those shrieked commands and underneath those commands the order *Feuer,* fire. Who can forget them, those screams and shots? That's why today when I meet Germans who are my age or older I avoid them. But I don't hate them. Then, in Yugoslavia, I hated them, I wished for their death."

I can't avoid the Americans, but they're not my enemies.

"You even have their blood in your veins," Nicola added. "Your grandmother wouldn't forgive you."

It's true, a quarter of my blood is American, but I never felt its presence. It got all dissolved in the Neapolitan cocktail.

"Nevertheless, you are part American," he continued, "and you keep quiet like a foreigner, not like us. When we keep quiet one can tell from our face what we're not saying. You keep quiet and one can tell you're in another place, like me with that family in Sarajevo, God bless them wherever they are, that I never managed to call by name because it was too hard to say, like all the words in their language."

One can see, Nicola, that I keep quiet in American.

During one of those afternoons a rare spectacle took place. The *Andrea Doria*, the transatlantic liner that made the crossing to America and had its home port in Naples, passed in front of the fishermen's beach. In the narrow stretch of sea between the island and the Vivara shoal the gigantic prow appeared, cutting off the channel used by the ferryboats. The island was dumbstruck. Usually, the ship slid past in the open sea, and you saw her at a distance. But this time she changed course and entered the channel between the islands. I was the first to spot her and I asked Nicola, "What is she doing?" Nicola sprang to his feet, told me to carry the tackle to the house, and called out to the other fishermen. The fishermen's beach was in an uproar, everybody dashing around. I did not understand what upset them so much. Those whose boats were anchored just beyond the beach raced out to board them and rowed out to deep water. Those whose boats were close to the beach called out to one another and helped one another drag them up on the sand as far back as possible. In the meantime, the ship approached the opening of the channel, the sea foaming white at the point of her keel. From the port, the harbor police sounded the siren in salute and the ship replied with the bellow of a monster. She crossed the channel and everything looked tiny compared with her height, even the castle. Her smokestack alone was the size of a palace. The boats that had managed to reach open water took the first waves. We saw them bounce on the huge crests and the fishermen turned into rodeo riders mounted on a beast that kicked its rump as high as the sky. Hit sideways, they would have been overturned. That was what I had not understood: the waves. They flung themselves against the beach with hurricane force, lifting the few boats still at anchor and hurling them at the shore, and on the beach the foam oozed all the way up to the houses. It was an onslaught of six enormous waves followed by a few smaller ones. The noise on the beach covered the last welcoming blasts of the sirens.

The fishermen were still calling out and helping one another. I had never seen so marvelous and so terrifying a mechanism at such close range. The waves reached the boats that had been beached and pulled two of them out to sea. Fortunately they did not collide with those that had been thrown against the shore and no damage was done. For the rest of the afternoon the fishermen worked together to clean up the mess, each helping the others. I helped too. Nicola thanked me for having noticed in time, because even a minute's delay could have wreaked havoc. When the other fishermen came to thank Nicola, he pointed to me and they wanted to offer me a glass of rosolio, a sweet wine.

I was appalled by the thought that this stupendous spectacle could be so dangerous to people whose livelihood was fishing. It had already happened before. Every so often, a transatlantic liner slid into the channel to provide the passengers on board with a view of the island, and created a five-minute storm with her waves, big enough to sink all the boats.

The fishermen weren't angry. A big ship also belonged to the sea, to the whirlwinds, to the storms, to all the fury of nature against which man pitted himself. You could see their patience from their mouths. After the waves and the work of putting the beach back in order, they stood around smoking their pipes, smiling over the success of their defenses.

Daniele's friends had been on the beach when they caught sight of the *Andrea Doria* and they swam out to the motorboat that belonged to one of them in order to meet the ship. They had run the risk of capsizing on the waves, but then they rode on the carpet of the wake, following the ship for a while. Under the stern they experienced a reverse vertigo, as if they were clinging to the edge of an abyss. These impressions were Caia's, always disposed as she was to visions and seeing things upside down. The thundering propeller made the sea boil in front of them and the ship's answering horn sounded to her like the holy day ram's horn of her childhood.

It was that same evening, after the ship's appearance, that we met by chance for the first time since her anger on the terrace over her name. She was heading for the beach, to the house where she was a guest. I was coming up from the fishermen's beach, covered with sand, oil, and grease like the boats after the near catastrophe. I saw her approaching and when she noticed me she ran up to me gaily, her curls bouncing in the air and her sandals sliding on the smooth road. She excitedly related the whole adventure, the thrills and the screams on the rearing motorboat, the disappointment when the waves subsided, the wonder of that white tabletop of flat sea produced by the immensity of the stern, and all the rest up to the ram's horn. She stopped at that reference to her childhood, which at the time I could not understand—the sound of the shofar in the synagogue on the occasion of Yom Kippur. I was unfamiliar with those holidays. She stopped, as she had in the middle of the dance floor, surely remembering her outburst and abrupt departure, but this time she looked at me differently, like a little girl at an old man. Even her voice lost its secure, enveloping tone and was replaced by a childlike trill. She saw how dirty I was, and reproached me for not making better use of my vacation, for spending too much time on fishing. I didn't want to tell her about the upheaval on the fishermen's beach and spoil her pleasure by injecting an afterthought of fear. I nodded my agreement. Yes, I knew how messy

I looked to her. I cleared my throat, gestured with my palms up to indicate the condition of my clothing, and said in a strange deep voice, "I'm sorry."

In a near whisper, almost without opening her lips, she said, "Let me hear my name again."

I looked at her, not at her eyes but a little higher, at the edge of her hairline where her thick chocolate strands lay flat and where I would have liked to plant a kiss.

"Chaiele," I said in a voice not my own.

"Again."

"Chaiele."

She closed her eyes, squeezing them hard, then opened them wide and said, "Try to make the *l* soft, let it melt in your mouth like candy," and she pronounced it for me. I repeated it. "That's how I was called, the way you said it now. I don't want to know how you found out. I don't want to tell you anything. You are not to say that name in front of the others. For them I am Caia. Only for you am I Chaiele. Do you understand?"

This time I closed my eyes and no longer saw that place on her forehead. I answered yes, in that strange deep voice that came from the bottom of my throat, the bass tones of a guitar. She kissed my cheek while my eyes were still closed.

"I love you very much Chaiele."

"I know," she said, stepping away. Then, changing her tone, she was Caia again. "Let's see you around, and get yourself cleaned up."

At the house I told Daniele about the waves on the beach, about Nicola's bravery and the way the men helped each other. He said nothing about the speedboat ride in the ship's wake. Perhaps he wasn't with them. He was dressed for tennis, having just returned from a game. We were both dirty from our island vacation, but our sweat was different. That evening I washed with fresh water and soap, emerging from the bathroom without a trace of salt on me. I told Daniele that now I needed a dip in the sea.

"Good idea," he replied. "I'll try to convince the others to go for a night swim."

I was happy to join them to get rid of my soapy smell. Mama intervened, asking Daniele if it wasn't unusual for a boy not to stay with boys of his own age. What was he doing in a group of older boys? Daniele replied that I was ahead of my age and that I was more comfortable with them.

"You really consider him one of your group?"

"You know him, Aunt, he starts talking to someone or stands around watching, and when he's had enough he goes off without even saying good-bye," he replied, pretending to be reproachful. It was a joke between us. It was summer, even if we were growing up in hard times, the postwar years. Those months on the island were a free port. Unimaginable liberties were allowed and each individual character could emerge and develop. Those of us who became adults after that time were more the products of an island than of the mainland.

eee

That evening I went out with a towel that my mother forced on me along with a sweater. The beach was dark. Light came from the lanterns of the fishing boats offshore, a stripe across the water. Daniele was already there with his crowd and he asked me to go back to the house to get the guitar. Those were the kinds of services asked of the newest member of a group, and it was natural for me to perform them, but Daniele asked with courtesy. Something was happening that summer. I was becoming another person in the eyes of others but I didn't know who. By the time I returned, they were already singing and there was wine. I didn't like wine but a glass was put into my hand in recompense for the guitar. I sat down outside their circle and wet my lips with little sips. The night was still. The water at the shoreline didn't seem to move at all. When it's like that it's no longer sea, it's like sky. On the dome above our heads the stars were clustered as thickly as granules, and in the pine forest the air stood still.

Daniele was singing one of his own songs which the others already knew, and in that very good passage of the refrain they sang along with him. Caia was next to a boy I had never seen before. When I finished my wine, I undressed and got into the smooth water. I moved carefully so as not to disturb the surface and with every frog kick I glided swiftly, meeting no resistance. I wound up swimming far out. Opening my eyes under the water, I saw a luminosity. By the time I understood what it was I was in its midst—a swarm of jellyfish. Feeling my hands on fire, I wheeled around and broke into the fastest stroke I possessed. I got away but I was covered with stings. Seeing the others in the water, I warned Daniele about the jellyfish which were moving toward the beach. Once on shore I checked my skin: like having fallen into a bed of stinging nettles, red welts everywhere except on the face. I dried myself in order to get dressed; my clothes weighed heavily on me.

In the meantime the luminosity had come closer to the shore and everybody got out of the water. Caia came out holding a boy's hand. Seeing me, she came up to me and quietly said, bending over me, "Don't judge me. I'm a girl and this is a summer holiday."

Of course I don't judge you, Chaiele, I'm on your side. I'm your serf, I'm the stage set behind you, I'm your worst dance partner, your guardian. All of this went through my head in response to her remark, but the only thing that came out as I offered her my towel was, "Don't catch cold, Chaiele," which only she could hear.

In reply, she whispered tenderly, "You, mine."

Turning back to the boy, she wrapped the towel around her shoulders. Mine were a hairshirt of needles, and above, the stars were a cluster of jellyfish. I must have had a fever to see them like that.

I went home and dropped on my bed stark naked. I heard Daniele come back in the middle of the night. He was astonished to find me still awake. He turned on the light and saw the grotesque red mottling.

"I wound up in the middle of them," I said.

"Jellyfish? Why didn't you say so right away, damn it, what did you put on?"

"Nothing."

He went to the bathroom, found a salve, and tried it out on one area. It felt better. I was grateful for his attentions. I fell asleep as he was saying, "One more day of this and you'd go back to the city in an ambulance."

eee

The next day he told me I had talked in my sleep. I was unable to pretend indifference. I was alarmed. I asked him what I had said. He didn't want to tell me and began teasing me. Then in a burst of laughter he admitted he hadn't understood one damn thing. I had been speaking in some invented language.

"You're a Ukrainian," was the first crazy thing that came to his mind. "You even had another voice, deep. I thought you might have caught cold."

In the morning it was raining. Low clouds dropped showers, got caught on the pines, then moved on. The streets on the island gleamed, the plants gave off a perfume of earth revived. The resin of the pines clung to the air, arousing a desire to make plans for the day—go up to the hills, go across the chestnut grove, or to the hot springs. The island was full of hot springs, even in the sea, near the shore. The rain announced that summer was waning. *"Aùsto capo 'e vierno,"* Nicola used to say, August is the beginning of winter.

I went to the fishermen's beach. Few of them had gone out, most stood in front of their houses amid the beached boats. They had pulled them up on the sand. I ran into Uncle, who had come to discuss the price of a new motor. It was a rare treat to spend time with him. After the negotiations, we said good-bye to Nicola and I accompanied Uncle all the way home. I had inherited the same name as his, a burdensome bequest. I had to calculate the distance between his accomplished manhood and my raw youth, exacerbated by my frequent silences. He must have thought that his nephew was no great tribute to his name. The old timidity I always felt in his presence, for once, that day, was on vacation. We talked about the next fishing trip, trolling for tuna and garfish which would close the season. The day was slow to end. I felt he was in a mood to chat and tried to get him to tell me something about the war.

First of all he said that trying to find answers from others is like wearing somebody else's shoes. Answers you have to find for yourself, made to your measure. Those of others are uncomfortable. He found my obsession with those years unhealthy.

"I would gladly have ceded them to you, I would have swapped with you, and in your place I wouldn't want to know a thing. For me, those years were torture."

He had hated to say "sir," had been ashamed of wearing a uniform, and often took it off at the risk of a court-martial. The eighth of September, the day of the armistice, was the day of deliverance. For him, fascism had been a scarecrow tarred black so as to be the opposite of leftist red. Until the disaster of the war he had regarded it as a tattered travesty of Roman history. Then fascism made the fatal error of taking itself seriously and mistaking itself for a warrior.

"My mother, your grandmother, Ruby Hammond of Birmingham, Alabama, gave me a taste for freedom, for individual worth, for making one's own way in the world. I could not have been born into a less fitting period. All those uniforms, rallies, party memberships were bad jokes repeated all day long. I stayed out of it as long as I could by going to France and Switzerland. My mother had taught all of us her English and the French of a proper upbringing. At that time it was rare, and a major advantage."

Even in Paris fascism nettled him. An agent tried to enlist him as an informer because he frequented Italian circles. Disgusted, he left Paris and transferred his business to Switzerland.

Then the war broke out, he was called up, he proffered excuses, delays, and finally had to put on the hated uniform.

"I saw no enemies and I shot no one. I know that's not enough for you, but it is for me."

Uncle had managed to remain detached from his time, to treat it with pure contempt, not for political reasons, but because of a natural, physical aversion. He had also managed to avoid suffering from isolation, an ill that befalls those who despise their own times. It was impossible to use him as a model. His was an elegance of mixed blood that glows for only one generation. We, the sons, grandsons of that grandmother, carried only vague traces of that successful crossing of an American and a Neapolitan.

えええ

Uncle shunned the reigning conformity of his contemporaries because of his very nature. He sabotaged fascism where it was most sensitive and most pathetic—in its virility—by bedding the wives and mistresses of officials, even famous ones. These things he did not tell me, they were known, handed down. I asked him if he had ever had enemies. There was someone who held him a grudge, the usual stories of adultery, he said, someone who wanted to shoot him, and he remembered an agitated scene in a hotel, right out of an operetta, with a friend of his who flung herself into the bed, taking the place of the other woman, minutes before the woman's lover burst into the room. Personally, he never considered anyone an enemy. He had, however, hated his uncle, who, on the premature death of his father, had taken over the business and had humiliated him, forcing him to leave. He had really hated him. He was young then and he was right to feel that way. Later he did not experience hostility.

"Not even toward the Germans?"

Not even them. Yes, he knew about the war and thought they had deserved a divided Germany and the Nuremberg trials. But he was one of the few soldiers in that war who had not known them. And so he couldn't feel hostile. Such feelings had to be awakened by personal experience, not history.

"To hate for political reasons, to hate in the abstract, is something I don't understand, something I don't know how to imagine." He spoke calmly as we wended through the island's alleys, avoiding puddles. For once we wore shoes because of the rain. Our feet were encased for the first time after weeks of going unshod and they clamored for air, earth, and sea.

"May I ask why the war interests you so much?"

I had no short, easy answers like the ones he gave. I only said, "Because it's your history, the only one we can learn from voices rather than from books." I could have added that it was the only one I could challenge, because there were still witnesses, victims who had survived, murderers in good health. And they could be found under the clothing of the tourists who came to bare themselves to the sun, and under the name of a foreign girl you could easily fall in love with, but none of the grown-ups taught you how to recognize those tourists, how to know what world you were in. I had to keep asking people who no longer wanted to give answers, and all the while history was sweeping away the dust along with the ashes of the cremated, forests grew over mass graves, all of life forged ahead, hiding what lay behind. And I was as stubborn as a mule but without reason, for mules rebel when the load is too heavy, whereas I had no load at all. If I had no reason, why then was I so stubborn? Because of love, no doubt, but also because of a snarl of torment and a touch of incipient rage—the froth of my rapid growth during that summer.

Uncle told me that enemies were bothersome, they required too much attention and emotion. Let someone else make the effort of being your enemy, of expelling the hatred in his body. And he squatted like someone sitting on a toilet, in part as a joke, because he liked to laugh and make fun of the silly, stupid things people do when they're being serious.

"You're too young to have enemies. How old are you, sixteen? You should find yourself a girlfriend. Daniele tells me that you hang around with his friends, but those girls don't give a hoot about you. They go for the older ones. You'd be better off going around with boys and girls your own age before the summer ends."

He was once again talking to a boy from the distance of an adult. I couldn't make him resume his previous manner, yet I had a tremendous urge to talk to him about Caia, ask him about her.

We had reached the gate where he was staying, a cool little cottage. For him the summer was a complete separation from his family. His work took him all over Naples, but when it came to vacations, he devoted his time entirely to himself. His wife was in the mountains with their other sons. Daniele, who preferred the sea, stayed with us. If I had talked

to him about Caia, about a girl, he would have remained with me longer, he would have talked to me
from his experience, would have taken me seriously,
because he took love seriously. He would certainly
have told Daniele later on. I had to forgo talking to
the one person who could have clarified my thoughts
and explained what was happening to me. He looked
up at the north wind that tore away the clouds, re-
vealing blue between the gaps, and said as he left,
"See you tomorrow when we go fishing." And he ex-
tended his hand to shake mine, a significant gesture
he had never made before. I was changing in his eyes
too, but I didn't know how, except for that cockeyed
one-sided love of mine.

୧୧୧

It would suddenly happen that my voice dropped,
and soon after changed back. It would happen that
my hands fell into a new position, folded under my
armpits like someone trying to warm up. It would
happen that I rubbed my nose with the back of
my thumb even though it didn't itch. I would ab-
sentmindedly make strange, pointless movements.
I had the impression of hearing Caia's voice from

far away, but she wasn't speaking Italian and yet I thought I understood her. Was I losing my mind? If that was the case, it wasn't so bad; on the contrary, it induced a kind of generalized love, not a desire for Caia's body, but merely to be near her, offer her my help, encourage her, cheer her up. I felt growing in me a maturity that gave rise to such thoughts as: You can count on me, I won't abandon you.

What could I possibly do for her, what kind of crazy ideas were taking shape in my head? The more I resisted them, the bolder and stronger they became. I felt the weight of many years. An intense feeling of shared intimacy kept my thoughts focused on Caia. I found myself moving more slowly. In her presence my breathing was even; away from her it was agitated. I would clasp my knees the way Uncle did and would stare at the design left by the moray's teeth. It was a tattoo, an indecipherable red letter.

I was changing for her. Caia was turning me into someone else and it wasn't just love that was involved. When I said to myself, "Chaiele, Chaiele," the tenderness of a father welled up in me, a father who had a little girl to bring up, to put to bed, leaving on the hallway light.

My body was as immature as before, but the life inside it raced ahead commanded from outside, from far away. I could feel the onset of an icy anger, kept under a control that did not diminish it but, on the contrary, kept it alert, like the nerves in my teeth when I sucked ice.

ele

One night I was allowed to go with Nicola to set the lines. A whole night on the sea. Daniele had gone once and did not recommend it. It was nothing but work, pitch-darkness, and silence. "You don't feel like saying a word, and it's not like night fishing when you go out for squid with lanterns. It's just a lengthy preparation for the next day's fishing." It was preparative work and I wanted to participate in it. In addition, I thought I might gather a bunch of impressions to bring back to Caia. Nicola generally left at ten o'clock and returned just before dawn to pick up Uncle and go back out with him at first light. In those intervening hours the fish were supposed to have hooked themselves on the long lines dropped to the bottom.

We left on the absolute calm of a summer evening. The bow of the boat did not move out of the sight line of the Forio shoal on the other side of the island. I held the rudder along the coastline while

Nicola cleaned the bait, then he took over the tiller.
In the dark he looked for the landmarks that indicate the shoal by their alignment. A lighthouse, the
light of a church, the twin-peaked outline of Mount
Epomeo: these were the landmarks that were supposed to come together in an angle three miles off
the island. Fishermen see the sea under a grid of
lines; they follow routes without a compass.

The darkness did not encourage an exchange of
words. Nicola remained silent as he groped around
in the dark. The moon had not risen, the sea was
empty, the sky aglow. Far offshore we came upon
two fishermen who were rowing back. Nicola pulled
up to them. Their motor had conked out. They lit a
kerosene lamp and Nicola went on board to lend a
hand. He was the most gifted mechanic in the fishing village. I put the oars in the water and stayed
close by. I heard their quiet talk mixed with the wash
of the oars, mere fragments of words because at sea
they understood one another from just the main syl-
lable, the accented one, a kind of stenography taught
by the wind which carried off the rest of the word.

I thought about that evening on land with Daniele and Caia not wishing to turn around and look at
the island. On the sea I did not feel distance. A third
of a moon rose, losing its red rind on the pavement

of still water. A powerful smell of bait filled the air now that we were stopped. With my fist I splashed the baskets with water. The wood of the oars fit snugly into the palm of the hand, legs placed one in front, one behind, to support the body's push on the oars: and so there I was conforming to custom, to the métier, to the hour of the night; there was a place for me in that vastness of the sea, a place to put feet and hands and do what was needed. Caia was solid ground, eternal woman in a century that held me by the throat out of love and rage, but not out there, not on the sea. There, I was in the commingled nights of the earth's numberless summers, I was a coeval of the planet, one of its wakeful species.

~~~

</center>

An hour passed before Nicola made a temporary repair. I pulled up alongside and we set out as the other boat went in. The men barely exchanged a good-bye.

We reached the shoal with a bit of aft wind. Nicola no sooner turned off the motor than he got busy with the line and the bait. The moon was small but bright. He threw in the signal buoy that had a strip of white cloth tied to the top of a stick. I was already at the oars, pushing off in the direction he called out. The boat moved swiftly and in the stern Nicola rapidly lowered the line of the rig with the bait attached. At the beginning of each coil he murmured a wish for top-quality fish in the morning: bass, porgy, grouper. We were making good progress and the wind cooled the work. I had to make an effort to turn my wrist when raising the oar out of the water because waves were coming up.

Halfway through, the moon disappeared and the wind picked up. Nicola was not smoking; not a good sign. I followed his directions: "Right," "Left," and the sea covered my labored breathing which was embarrassing me. When Nicola lowered the last float with the flag on top, the wind blew it out straight. The waves were growing heavier and I was exhausted. The motor kicked in; it was two o'clock and we were drenched from the spray.

The sea came over the bow, the crests of the waves were ripped off by the gusts of wind. I had brought along a light woolen sweater which was already soaked, but Nicola told me to put it on even so. We no longer spoke. With a pail I bailed out the water that came in over the sides. The darkness augmented the swelling sea and the shock of the waves. In a storm, the sea is not a plain but a hill full of ditches. The island had vanished behind the wind.

A breach was opening between the impressions I would have liked to describe to Caia and the raw experience that shuts down the senses and ignites the instinct of survival. I was no longer capturing fireflies in my fist to show a girl, I was under the yoke of a job that had to be seen through to the end. I scraped the bottom of my resources in the hope of finding more. My strained scrawniness was wearing to a thread over the empty lines. Nicola kept to his tiller and became part of the boat, more mast than man.

At the top of a long wave Nicola saw the glimmer of the boat of the two fishermen. It was adrift. They had given up on the oars, useless against that wind, and the repair had not held up under all the battering. They had sought refuge under the small shelf in the bow where tackle was stored. Nicola came up on the windward side and shouted to them to come out and be ready to catch a rope. It seemed to me at once that if we towed them, we wouldn't budge in that sea, that even without them we were barely moving. But there was nothing else we could do. The fishermen would not abandon their boat and it was impossible to bring them aboard ours.

Their gestures told the whole story: Nicola would try to tow them and they would cut the rope if our boat couldn't make it. The only thing they said to each other was, "Catch!" The rope wound up in the water but they managed to grab hold of it with a harpoon.

And so there we were at sea, smashing into waves, drenched, deafened by the wind, and I couldn't figure out whether we were moving or not. Nicola asked me if I felt up to working, not saying at what. Yes, I was, to combat the cold. He then altered the angle of our course so that we took the sea less from the bow than from the side and started taking on water. I later understood that Nicola was trying to enter into the lee of the island, abandoning the return route in the hope of finding a less exposed stretch of sea. For the moment, the effect was that the storm hit us broadside. I was bailing out seawater by the bucketful, which at least kept me warm. The fishermen in the other boat were doing the same. I kept losing my balance. In the raging blackness of the night I heard the clipped syllables of Nicola's voice at my shoulders: *"Né paù,"* the linguistic remains of *"Non aver paura,"* don't be afraid. Without turning around, I moved my head from side to side to indicate no.

Until then I hadn't even thought about it. Had he been afraid, I would have been more so, but so long as he remained at the tiller and set the course, fear did not touch me. I had no experience of storms, I did not know the degrees of danger, and certainly there was much worse than this. I took the punches of the sea and the yanking of the bucket on my back without knowing how much longer the boat could stay afloat. I was with the best in the trade, on their routes, in one of their nights. Fear of capsizing was far from my thoughts.

A wave filled the boat above our ankles. Nicola straightened the bow into the knots of wind to give me a chance to bail, then turned her back to getting hit broadside. This happened repeatedly. So long as that sea lasted, my strength would last, measured out to arrive at parity.

I first became aware that night was changing to dawn when we reached the leeward side of the island. The blended fragrance of sand, pines, and gardens wafted from the land to sea, stronger than the smell of coffee from a kitchen. The island was a dark cup that sent its aroma out to sea. I straightened up and heard again, this time from a broken voice, barely audible, *"Né paù,"* don't be afraid, and I turned to shake my head no and look him in the face. During the entire storm I had not seen him. He was soaked and as ashen as the dawn.

At last the sun rose and the eight hundred meters of Mount Epomeo broke the headwind enough to calm the sea. As we arrived in the bay of Sant'Angelo, the first sound we heard from the land was a bell calling the faithful to mass. Touching the ribs of my back, I felt proud to have worked throughout a storm. There was no pride, however, in the expressions of the fishermen; for them that night was just another night of work, of going out for bread, and how dearly they paid for it. Passing my hand over my face to close my eyes and mouth, I wiped the pride from it, repressing the impulse to talk about that night. I did not listen to the remarks exchanged between the fishermen. They untied the tow rope and pulled out the oars. Only then did I see the olive branch above the prow of the boat. It had remained in place.

We disembarked at the small pier to notify Uncle at the other cape of the island that we couldn't reach him. Once on land, my feet on warm solid ground, I turned toward the side of the island where Caia was sleeping at that hour. I would not be relating my little boy's storm to her.

eee

My coevals no longer greeted me. But there was among them one fifteeen-year-old girl whose eyes followed me whenever I came by their group. Only the summer before I would have jumped hoops for a glance from her. I was sorry about the poor timing that kept desires apart instead of making them meet. I would have liked to explain myself to her but I didn't have the nerve to go up to her. I exchanged glances with her when our paths on the island crossed unavoidably.

One afternoon I saw her walking alone on the fishermen's beach. It was not the path one would normally take for a walk or a place one would go to expressly. I was sitting with my back to the sea in front of Nicola when I saw her approach, looking all around. She had on a peasant dress and a man's sandals, and her freshly washed fair hair fell loosely. I waved to her and she greeted me, stopping at a distance. Not knowing what to do, I stood up and she came toward me. I introduced her to Nicola. "Pleased to meet you Eliana," he said, apologizing for not extending his dirty hand. She took it anyway, by the back of his hand, and it became obvious that all three of us were ill at ease. I asked her where she was headed. She shrugged her shoulders to indicate no place in particular, and before I had a chance to wish her a nice walk she asked me to come with her. "All the way to there?" I asked, copying the gesture she had made. She smiled, yes. We said good-bye to Nicola and started walking toward the castle where the island's paths end.

We walked through the narrow streets of the village, I barefoot and scruffy, she clean and groomed. I explained my desire to learn about fishing, and told her that I was hanging out with the older group that summer because of my cousin Daniele, but even with them, as with those of my own age, I felt out of place. She suddenly took my hand and held it as we walked.

"I shouldn't be holding your hand, I've already made it dirty. I've changed and don't even know how. I have the thoughts of a man, about having children, working, leaving school. I'm suddenly in a hurry to learn other things. I can't come for you at school with a motorbike, which I don't have and don't want. I can't take you to Saturday night parties, be introduced to your parents as your boyfriend, hear them say yes, indeed, he's a nice boy. I'm not a nice boy. A short while ago I didn't know that as well as I do now."

She looked straight ahead, concentrated on a thought that pinched her eyebrows and furrowed her forehead. She let a few steps go by in silence, then answered that she did not know what was happening to her. She had known me earlier and had no interest in me or in the other boys. She said she was bored with the routine of the group, with the novelty of declarations of love that proliferated out of contagion or rivalry. She had begun to notice me out of a need to look for something new, and then the younger crowd accused me of playing the big shot by choosing to hang out with my cousin's friends. Her voice became constricted and she left off that little bit of singsong often heard in the speech of young adolescents: "I want to try to be with you. I want to believe it's possible, even if it's not for now, even if it's far off. I need to wait for someone who's different from the others, and you are that someone."

From a ground-floor kitchen came the smell of frying shrimp, followed, as we walked on, by the fragrance of a basket of figs on the terrace. I breathed it all in, even her voice. I gave her back the hand I had withdrawn. She took me back in time, to a time that was right for my age, coming on to me with a line a nice girl of the fifties would figure out. We walked without talking up to the entrance of the castle where the island juts into the sea like a turret.

"I left a grease spot on your palm. Let me try to get it off."

There were pumice stones among the rocks of the isthmus and I went down to find one. I rubbed her palm gently and saw her eyes start to fill.

"Am I hurting you?"

"No."

"Then don't look so unhappy."

"I'm not unhappy."

The first two tears fell, coming as they do in pairs, which is how poets learned to rhyme. I caught them on the pumice stone and wiped away the dirt on her hand. "Hurrah, it works," I joked to make her smile, and she did, wrinkling her nose.

We remained hand in hand with a piece of pumice stone between them. She was inviting me to an age that had disappeared from my body and my mind. She told me not to give her an answer. It was true that in our silence I was thinking about an answer. She told me to put her out of my thoughts, to let her wait. She had discovered that she liked the idea of waiting. She was no longer a kid the way she said these things, nor was she talking to one. It was as though there were someone between us, as though a postman were rapidly delivering the letters that we were sending each other. I told her this in search of some fable to explain what was happening to us. Then she said that the island was the postman, that we had explored it as children going on foot from house to house, and all at once, in a single summer, it was an undiscovered island. We were the only ones on that strip of land, we had lost our city and our age, and we were emerging from our green shell like walnuts in September. I no longer know whether these were her words or whether that was how it sounded in the tube between the ear and the brain. Then, looking beyond me, she added, "I've never come to the fishing village before."

And I had never gone for a walk with a girl. I saw a spot of white on her lips and commented on it: "Around here they compare a girl to a fig when it ripens and oozes a drop of milk. 'Ianchéa,' meaning that it's white." I had thought of the milk of a fig when I touched her tears. They had the power to grow, the impulse to become a woman, they had fallen all swollen. I was glad I had collected them. She stood up first.

"It did me good to come here, to talk to you. I feel stronger now. Before I came, I was very nervous."

She looked around, was reassured, took a firm step and laced her arm through mine, not taking my hand this time. Her sandals squeaked of new leather, the north wind blew her hair forward, covering her face. She said nothing more. We adjusted our stride to walk in step, pleased to be on a route of return.

"You've been a friend to me today. I'm an elephant and won't forget it."

She did not come again. As she walked away, she waved friendly good-byes and gave me toothy smiles.

ee

The days were getting busy, departures imminent, occasions to meet desperately desired. I did not want to count the time, but it was short. And so I began to look for Caia, hoping to find her alone. That's when the meetings came to pass. She was coming from the sea with her sandals in her hand, her feet all sandy, when she saw me and I made a brusque gesture with my arm the way one hails a bus at a bus stop. It wasn't a greeting, it was a reflexive jerk, out of place. We were face-to-face; she scrutinized me carefully and spoke to me as though continuing a conversation begun earlier.

"I used to call my father *Tateh*. In our language at home, Yiddish, it means papa. You just made a gesture that my father used to make at the school bus that brought me home every day. I would look for him at the window and he was always there waiting for me. It was my first year of school. You made the same gesture and I felt chills go down my spine. See, I have goose bumps. This is not the first time I see something of my father in you."

I remained immobile, trying to stay still, forcing myself to refrain from any gesture, resisting the urge to make nervous movements that were forcing themselves on me. I did not want to yield to the temptation of blindly imitating unfamiliar gestures. I drew a breath and rubbed the back of my index finger under my nose to scratch it, even though it didn't itch.

"That was one of my father's tics when he was nervous. He rubbed his finger as you did and squeezed his eyelids. What are you doing to me?"

"I don't know, Caia," I said, making myself pronounce her name in the open, keep my distance, keep from embracing her, and keep myself from crying. The sun was out, I was happy to have found her, I could walk her home, tell her about the fishing trip, ask for her address to send her a letter or two when the summer was over, so why the hell did I want instead to cry, to hug her, to make a scene in the middle of the street?

She saw my confusion, which made me clasp my hands behind my back to keep from gesturing, saw me flounder, and then she smiled and came beside me. She took my arm and spoke with a touch of emotion that made her voice metallic: "Why you? I know there are moments when someone I lost comes close and inhabits an unfamiliar person, just for a moment, to greet me through the body of another person with an unmistakable movement or signal, just a signal, that's all. I've known for a long time that I haven't been left alone. You can call them fantasies, my need to believe, and you may be right. But I feel protected by this multitude of hardly perceptible signals. Until now, no one has ever brought together so many of them. They come from my father who is no more, but I don't want to talk about him with anyone, not even with you. They come from my father and you are becoming his puppet, and I feel like asking him to stop it, to leave you alone."

"No, Chaiele, I don't want to be left alone. I don't know what's been happening to me in this brief period since I got to know you, but it's a fulfillment.

It's not just the love of a bewildered kid, it's anger against an evil I don't know, or know by only a few names, it's that I see you so alone you need someone to look after you, and that someone is me, an ordinary kid who feels the weight of years just because he happens to be near you. I don't know how to tell you I love you because the only spot I'd like to kiss is where your forehead begins, under your hair."

"Do it, do it! There's no point telling you that's where he used to kiss me."

We stopped walking and I placed my palms on her temples and kissed the top of her forehead and I started to cry with a voice not my own, saying without rhyme or reason, "So much time, Chaiele, so much time." Like an old man at a train, that's how I cried, quietly, without sobbing, tears falling softly on the window, falling on Caia from my cheekbones, and she said: "It's me, *Tateh,* your Chaiele, I know you never left me, I know, don't cry, you are with me, always, leave this boy, let him have his own age, we're something else, he can't know, and yet he offered himself to you and me. I know, that time at the train you let me leave alone, but I didn't cry then or even now, because I knew that you would find me, and so you did. You appeared behind so many faces, yet I always recognized you."

Then she spoke in a language I had never heard and it was a cascade of words fit for a lullaby. And so I stopped crying and raised my lips from her forehead and my hands from her temples. I took her by the arm and walked her to the door of her house and watched her climb the stairs, turn to wave good-bye, and add that gesture of hailing a bus. I was left with rinsed eyes, a feeling of calm in the palm of the hand that had touched the pulsing of her veins, and the most absurd tenderness I had ever experienced, just from the sound of that name, *Tateh*.

ᏋᏋᏋ

She no longer reproached me for having infiltrated her secret. She had entrusted me with a name, a piece of her heritage. I had placed a kiss at the top of her forehead and she accepted it. She did not become angry as she had that evening on the terrace when she thought she had heard me say her secret name, Chaiele. I forgot to ask her address, but it didn't matter. Even without letters I had a place close to her and a name, *Tateh,* that came from a time before I was in the world and awaited me on an island to be pronounced. So long as I was near her everything seemed natural, but away from her I did not understand the story of Caia and her father. I was aware only of the good fortune of serving as a bridge to her childhood. I could feel how much she depended on that bridge and on me. And I could feel growing in me a severity that contained both blessings on life and curses on the evil perpetrated against that life, and a serenity coupled with an urge to bang my fist on the table.

That's why what happened afterward was the inevitable consequence of her childhood and of my precocious aging which had resulted from having met Caia. It had to happen that night in a pizzeria where Daniele's friends were having a farewell dinner before separating one by one in the departures to follow. And it had to be that I was there too.

e e e

It was an evening of repressed high spirits that erupted in bursts, not choral and steadily rising, but nervous, self-indulgent: someone laughed by himself till the tears came, another drank one glass too many, someone else tried to find the right tone to take leave of the island and of the others. Toasts were proposed to all the different kinds of fish. Few other clients were in the pizzeria when a group arrived.

The owner seated them on the terrace where we were. They may already have eaten, since they only ordered drinks.

No one paid them any attention except me. They were middle-aged Germans, men and women, about fifteen of them. Our dinner was in full swing and we were making noise. We were deciding where to go afterward and wild proposals were being made that increased the racket. The sound of clinking glasses and a few loud remarks began coming from the Germans' table. Caia looked distracted and was staring in the direction of the sea. Someone called out to her, asked her how she thought they should spend the rest of the evening, and for a moment she was back among them with an answer. But her thoughts were elsewhere, perhaps on the forthcoming departures, or the interruption of the summer's friendships by the return home.

From the other table came the humming of a song. Caia stiffened and looked far off, above the heads. When that song ended, another began, a kind of march. Daniele became aware of Caia, of her tenseness, and asked her something. He had barely touched her when she sprang to her feet and began shouting in German at the people sitting at the next table. Her voice was clear and sharp, and rose above their singing. Daniele and the others fell silent in astonishment at the peal of her voice assaulting strangers. They did not understand what was happening. Daniele turned to see at whom Caia was shouting. They went on singing but were listening, and a few of them stopped. All of them were looking at her. She was aflame, a fire no one had ever seen before or understood. Her outburst ended in a shriek, a wounded rage that must have contained some terrible insult because at the other table the chorus stopped dead and they began shouting, and one of them got up amid a clatter of chairs. Still lacking any understanding of what was going on, Daniele jumped up, knocking over his chair, and grabbed one of them. He moved instinctively, accurately, and tackled him, knocking him to the ground. I fell on the second one who was about to intervene, taking him by surprise from the side and rolling him over the table. It turned into a free-for-all. From either side people tried to break it up, the owner came running, as did people in the street. It didn't last more than a minute; more noise than punches. Caia remained riveted to her final shriek, rigid, absent from the ruckus. During the confusion the other group wound up near the exit and began to leave the place. Our group got busy straightening up.

Daniele explained that the Germans had insulted us, so the owner did not call the police, seeing that we were decent kids, good clients. In the end, nothing happened.

Caia gave no reply to those who asked her what those insults were. She kept her eyes closed. Someone had already started to tease her, saying that of all the ideas for how to spend the rest of the evening, this was one no one had thought of and they could make the rounds of the pizzerias with this new gimmick. Daniele adjusted his shirt. His knuckles were scraped from the first punch and everybody told him he had done the right thing, and he went over to Caia, who finally loosened up and smiled at him. She said nothing, but took him by the arm and led him outside. The beach—they were all going to the beach to make a bonfire, and they would have to look for me to ask for the guitar, for I was no longer there.

℮℮℮

I was invaded by a rage I had never felt before, a whiff of heat in my nostrils, a wrath that had made me explode with Daniele in the melee and that had not subsided. It was growing stronger and filling me. Caia's scream had inflamed my nerves, like a whiplash to my spinal cord, more the strike of a snake than a man. Never was I so quick to act. I did something perfectly serene and awful: I followed the Germans. I followed them from a distance. In my ears I heard the buzzing of flowering, as when insects swarm on a tree in bloom.

They stopped at a bar and drank for an hour, without singing. I waited for them and followed them all the way to a pensione outside the center of town. I didn't know why I was doing that, I was obeying the whiff of heat but without tension, careful not to be seen. I turned around and rejoined the group on the beach. They were in a circle singing, facing the fire, already hoarse. For the first time they took notice of me. Someone had told Daniele that I too had thrown myself into the melee. They greeted me with a genuine welcome and one of them said that the team was now complete and they could go pick a fight at some bar. Caia had regained her cheerfulness, and was singing. She invited me to sit beside her. When they started to sing a new song she said, talking directly to me, "You were brave to defend me. No one has protected me in a long time, and I am grateful to you for having done so. In one part of my anger there was the reassurance that you were there. They were singing the anthem of the SS, you don't know it, I do.

I heard it for the first time when the first Germans arrived and my father was carrying me in his arms and holding me tight. I did not hear it again during my childhood. I can't tell you I'm sorry for what happened because I'm happy it happened."

The music covered her words. Daniele was singing his most popular song, strumming chords with his skinned knuckle. Ignited by her eyes on me, I replied calmly, "I don't know what you shouted, but your voice seemed to come from a height, from a place far above our heads. In a kind of hallucination I saw you standing in a burning house, shouting at the sky, not at the earth. All I did was follow Daniele, who jumped up to defend you."

"I saw, but what you're saying isn't so. You got up first and pushed the one who was coming at me, then Daniele got involved."

❧❧❧

The sequence of a brawl always has more than one version, so I don't know whether her memory was more accurate than mine. I happened to add, while the others were singing the refrain, "Chaiele, I have been ready for this for a long time. I have been waiting all my life for the chance to protect you."

When you stood up, I watched you at first, saw you get angry, and without understanding why, I obeyed you by getting angry too. When you spoke German to those people, I was already at your disposal. You were speaking to them but with my body in between. You were talking and I was ready to throw myself at them. These things I couldn't tell you.

"I never knew how my father died, but tonight I peeked into a room of the past. It may have been you who showed me how he died, jumping up to protect his wife the way you did with me. I saw many things tonight and I was afraid for you. I still am."

I unconsciously rubbed my nose with the back of my index finger and hastily stopped. I said to myself, "No, no," and Caia understood *"Nu, nu,"* an interjection in the language of her family.

"Nu, nu . . . you know that too, you, mine."

"Oi, Chaiele, we will not see each other again."

"Nu, Tateh, we will see each other again and again, without this boy who served us as a bridge and who bent like a bow over the span of our ages."

The music of the circle of voices droned on even though Daniele had stopped playing. What remained was the center, a bush of embers reflected on the hands, in the eyes. Somebody fell asleep, the others talked in twos and threes, Caia and Daniele. They were going to leave together for the city, then he would take her to the train station. I left them. For once I said good night to all of them, one by one, shaking hands, exchanging a kiss or two. Some were leaving the next day, Daniele and Caia soon after. In a few days I would be left alone. I went to the pensione where the Germans were. It was late, everything was quiet, the street empty.

I looked at the little garden behind the gate. In front there was a car with a German license plate. I wondered how to hurt them and a host of ideas came, stupid ones and criminal ones, all jumbled together, and I eliminated them one by one for want of means. I stayed there about twenty minutes and no one passed by to shatter the dark with a flashlight. Few streets on the island were illuminated. I went home and fell asleep, placidly mulling over the most horrendous thoughts that had ever entered my head.

I did not hear Daniele come home.

ℰℰℰ

In the morning I found a note: "Wake me, I'm coming fishing with you." It was hard to rouse him from a sleep that doubtless had scarcely begun. He got up grunting, panting from the effort of trying to understand that it was dawn, that we were going fishing, and that it was he who had asked me to come along. We started off barefoot on stone damp with dew. He was coming because he had to tell me, couldn't wait: "You knew that Caia is Jewish?" I replied with a curt no, the way you discard in a game when it's not the right suit. "She told me last night, or rather tonight, that is, just a little while ago, since I came to bed at three o'clock. That's why she got mad at those Germans. They were singing Nazi anthems. I'd never seen her so tense, so fierce. I really liked seeing her standing there all alone against that table of Germans. I thought they were insulting us and she was defending us, then I heard the noise behind me and I found my-self grappling with one of them. I learned later that you threw yourself on one of those animals. Only tonight talking with her did I understand why that uproar broke out. I knew nothing about Caia. It seems she lost her parents during the war."

Daniele wanted me to share his surprise and I was sorry not to, sorry to remain aloof when he had come to me as a friend and confided in me. But I couldn't say anything about what had happened to Caia and me, or what was percolating in my head. Not wanting to appear cold and wanting to reciprocate with a confidence, I told him I had fallen in love with her.

"I guessed as much but it seemed to me absurd for you to have any expectations. However, later on I did see you talking together. Not even to you did she say anything about her family, so you can't have been very close. In any case, I won't say anything to the others. I told you because I think you have a right to know. She came here among us this summer and turned everybody's head, including a few adults. She could at least have confided in you. You ran the risk of getting your head bashed in last night. Instead she kept everything to herself."

There was something reproachful about his remarks and I took it badly that Daniele should criticize her for my sake.

"Caia spared us. She suffered things that can never be told adequately. She didn't want to tell us, boys on a summer holiday on an island, who know nothing about Jews or Germans. We're too young. She was also too young, but they took everything from her. All of us, not just me, even the adults, are too young for her. She learned that she should say nothing. She talked with you tonight because you defended her better than anyone else, giving her courage and justification. She thanked you by telling you what kind of abyss lay below her anger. It's not fair for us to reproach her."

Daniele did not agree. Over the course of one summer he had observed a lovely girl, a bit capricious, who had danced and had been kissed by many and who, contrary to appearances, carried within herself a deep ache and a dark secret, and by sheer chance, because of a brawl, opened up to one person. "Better if she had told me nothing."

Really, Daniele? Is it really better that even at the very end we should not get to know someone we have had the chance to meet? We can identify the fish in the sea and the stars in the skies, but we should know nothing about the people on earth?

"No, that's not what I think; as a matter of fact, I'm grateful to her."

Even in this Daniele was generous. He was capable of correcting himself and yielding to someone else's opinion.

"She made me feel more grown up, she honored me with her trust. But what a girl! Too complicated for me. I'm used to this beautiful island, to fishing boats, guitars, vacations. And out of nowhere, someone's devastated life erupts in this blissful sleepy place, someone who seems to be like us."

"Yes, Daniele, she seems to be like us, yet she can't even tell us about her life."

The rock under our feet ended and gave way to the beach. We boarded the boat and Daniele, exhausted, stretched out under the morning sun, falling soundly asleep on the wooden planks as though on a bed. Uncle started to grumble, "What's the point of coming here if you need to sleep? What the devil do you do at night?" His plural "you" included me, even though I was wide awake and preparing bait. What annoyed him was to be unable to speak to his son, whose sleep he found disrespectful. He associated me with him in his reproach and he may have been right. I explained that it had been a farewell party, many were leaving today, but that did not placate him.

"In that case, stay home in bed. In the boat we fish."

There were many lines to pull up and a need for arms and hands so that Daniele was awakened. Uncle noticed Daniele's skinned knuckles.

"You got into a fight last night?"

"With some drunk Germans, but it was over very fast and nobody got hurt," Daniele answered to end the discussion.

Uncle was not in an indulgent mood. "Surely you know, you who are so mature and grown up, that brawling is a criminal offense, that you can tarnish your record for a scuffle in the street." He was angry. He reprimanded us for the way we lived on the island, for turning into savages; the vacation was too long, we were destroying ourselves with all that freedom. "If the police had come by, you would have been in deep trouble." He vented his ill humor on both Daniele and me. In the meantime Nicola had started to retrieve the first float and handed the line to Uncle, knowing that would calm him down.

He stopped grumbling and began pulling up the cable and soon felt the weight at the bottom, a resistance, and the fight to capture the grouper began. Once the fish came on board, all other concerns faded and all thought was focused on the sea, on the hooks, on the laborious retrieval of the rig's cable over a difficult shoal. Daniele's hands were bleeding slightly, the salt doubtless making his scraped knuckles burn in the sun, but he paid no attention to them; his palms, no longer used to handling the cable, surely burned even more.

I was a good day; Nicola took home a fine grouper for his family, good humor was restored. Uncle asked Daniele for a few details about the fight and was relieved to hear that we hadn't been clobbered. Daniele didn't say a word about Caia.

ℓℓℓ

While Uncle was grousing about the consequences of a brawl, I was elsehere. My thoughts went back to that pensione, to the need to find a way to attack without delay. What could I do? Throw rocks at the car, puncture the tires, break a window? The stupid pranks of delinquents. I was writhing in my impotence while my hands were busily occupied with fishing, aware that there was little time, for the Germans could suddenly take off. I had to decide on something that very day. Nothing came to mind, for which I reproached myself, but I told myself that I had never before thought of doing harm to anyone, and then I started all over again. There was a calm on the sea and inside of me as well, a calm that rippled up from below. On the way back Nicola said the wind was blowing up from the south.

As we left the fishing area, rockets celebrating a saint's day were exploding in the sky. The island was announcing the day of its protector with blasts as well as bells. Shots were fired into the air, exploding high up with a single powerful burst. To thank the saints on their name days we aim our antiaircraft battery at them. It may be a salute, but it's still a barrage against the sky.

A fantasy more than an idea came to me: a bunch of rockets going off in front of the pensione. I imagined the shock, the flight, the arrival of firemen. The thought of firemen sent a jolt through me. As we reached the shore, I jumped off the boat. I had found a way to strike. Fire, *Feuer.* That word had remained in Nicola's head: *Feuer,* fire, easy and violent. I had found it. The urge to act accelerated my thoughts and arranged them into a plan. I knew at once that I had to obtain a rubber tube. I cut it from the garden hose. I went to the pensione and saw that the foreign car was not there, but that was normal at that hour, noon. I brazenly asked if they had any rooms available. They had none. There would be some in three days. I had time.

From the moment I decided on fire, all objections were banished from my thoughts. The only thing that mattered was to succeed. I didn't care about being caught. I had become a guard, watching the enemy. I was no longer a boy. I got hold of a demijohn. I would fill it at night with gasoline siphoned from the tank of my father's car; at that time he was vacationing with us. I had seen Nicola do this on the boat. I succeeded on my first try without even getting any gas into my mouth. I was carrying out the actions of a plan, they came to me easily, effortlessly. I knew that a single match might not be enough to ignite the gasoline, so I put aside a whole box and a newspaper. Now I could strike at my choosing. I would do it after Caia and Daniele left so as not to implicate them, even marginally. I needed to be alone in my room the night I went out with a fire in my pocket. They were not to know. This was my thing, mine alone, sprung from the body of a boy during one brutal summer of love and rage.

There was a festival on the island that day, it was Caia's last evening. We were to go to the fair together and walk around the stands.

eee

First I went to the fishermen's beach. Nicola was getting the boat ready for the next night. For him there were no holidays, he would rest during the winter when there are days the sea doesn't want anybody on its surface. I gave him a hand. The other fishermen were already at the fair in their clean shirts, their only holiday attire. Nicola felt like talking to me, selecting words from both Neapolitan dialect and Italian.

"You're growing up. In one summer you've become a man. I heard on the boat that Daniele's fists were flying. Were you there too?" Yes, I said. "It's good to stand up for yourself, not let yourself be insulted. I can't hit anybody. As a boy, yes, but not since the war." I asked him if he had ever had enemies.

"I was in a place where the enemy was us. We were the enemies of a people who had done nothing to us and we were armed to occupy their territory. We were allies of the Germans against those people and we were wrong to be there. I was ashamed to make war against those people. When it was over and we lost, my shame disappeared all at once. My allies were that family who received me and hid me, bless them wherever they may be. I understood nothing about enemies."

But at that time he had enemies, didn't he? Didn't he wish them dead?

"When the Germans began losing, I saw them run away and die, and when I saw the slain body of an enemy, it was no longer an enemy. It wasn't anything. When we are corpses we are all alike. Even enemies die crying for help. They too burst open when they're shot, and the hatred, if you really had it inside of you, is no longer there. I saw dead enemies and I felt nothing. There are no enemies, it's all a mistake and you realize that once they're dead."

His voice was calm. I was flattered by his confidences. I was calm too, carefully weighing the words that came out of my mouth. The choice of fire had settled my nerves.

Nicola had seen enemies die and on seeing them had discovered that his body was emptied of hate. I understood that he had arrived at some conclusion, but he could not pass it on to me. His experience was not enough, was not able to save me from my own, or avert it. It was not for me to contradict him with arguments or attribute to him enemies he had known before me and better, people who had participated in the massacres of defenseless victims and who continued to enjoy their vacations in good health and without consequences. That was my conclusion, my premise. He continued to be tormented by the consequences. His words could tell me in advance how I would feel afterward, but they could not stop me.

I had wanted to break open Caia's secret; it had taken complete hold of me. I had taken her mourning as my banner. I had covered all the stations of love, from a kid with a crush on an older girl to a father who returned to protect her. From that fantasy of Caia's about her *tateh*, I realized that was how I really felt: like a father who comes back to find his daughter after many years, an emigrant who can once again embrace his child. Among the similarities she kept discovering between her father and me, the only one I shared was that particular emotion of a diffuse, mature love, now somber with anger.

 invalid

In the sky the rockets of the saints were exploding. An uncontrollable reflex made Nicola lower his head. He quickly raised it again but at the next explosion ducked once more. I kept my head up, knowing nothing about gunfire or how one feels under the real thing. My anger looked on the pyrotechnic artillery of the festival as a good omen. My anger was arrogant compared with the recoil from the blasts that bent Nicola's neck, his physical memory of attempts against his youth exposed to a bomb-filled sky.

"They were not like us, each one of them saw himself as part of a larger body. They were proud of that body. They obeyed the way a finger obeys the brain. They were no longer men as we understand them but men like replacement parts. They only felt right in uniform. They called prisoners *pieces* when they counted them. All other peoples were inferior to them, including us Italians. We were under their orders, but there were some awful things they couldn't make us do. We remained men, soldiers by force who couldn't wait to take off their uniform, stop fighting, return to work. I kept thinking about the fishnet that had cost me a year's work and was still new. And I ached with jealousy to think that someone else might use it, that my wife might sell it in order to eat. She didn't. During my hours off duty I fished in the river with a rod. I suffered so much heartache then, that ever since I never wanted to use a rod again. I used to bring my catch to my adoptive family, bless them wherever they are."

He was eager to explain himself and searched for expressions in Italian that he translated from Neapolitan. He shook his head from the strain. I was receiving a legacy of words that I stored in the jumble of my thoughts and in the confusion of my desperate need to reply.

To change the subject I asked him if he was going to the festival. I would be going later with Daniele.

"Me too, later, I'm taking the family."

ℯℯℯ

Those of the group still remaining on the island had made a date to meet and pushed into the festival as a

tight unit. All the inhabitants came to stroll through
the few streets. It was early evening; the lanterns
strung along the way made the sky pale. Caia held
my arm and complimented my clean shirt. "I have
shoes on too," I said, mockingly showing off my sandals. I saw that chipped piece of tooth emerge, making her smile all the broader.

The crowd broke up our group. The two of us
clutched each other's arms to avoid being separated.
Caia asked me to buy her a cone of cotton candy.
To be heard over the clamor, she raised her voice
in a child's squeal. She grasped the cone, plunged
her face into it, and finished it in a flash. I removed
the little granules of sugar stuck to her cheeks. She
was joyful the way one is when a childish mood
comes over a grown person, when a child's wriggle
takes hold of the feet, making them want to scamper
about. She pulled my arms, trying to run right into
the mob. I pretended to struggle, to be panting for
air, and wiped the palm of my right hand across my
temples all the way to the back of my neck. At one
point, she shook her head and whispered in my ear,
"*Tateh,* I know you're here, there's no need for any
more signs."

Her game with me struck me funny and brought
forth a throaty laugh I had never heard from myself

before. It was warm, slow, and came in short bursts. I felt it deep inside, heavy, filled with affection for my little Chaiele in the midst of the festival. She heard my laughter and instantly leaned her head against my shoulder. Above us the explosions started up again, no louder than champagne bottles uncorked in the sky.

She tried the shooting gallery, firing a compressed air gun at balls in a cage. Then she wanted a little doll no bigger than her hand, and I remembered to buy a cork for the demijohn. We came across Nicola and his family. I greeted him from a distance, but he didn't notice me. Then we ran into my father, who in his distraction and without his glasses greeted only Caia. She laughed because not even my father recognized me. I was transformed and no one knew who I was.

"Tonight only I know who you are at this festival."

"I'm *Tateh*?"

"Yes."

"Of course I'm *Tateh*. Tonight I am your father and you are my little Chaiele, and I know how to say your name the way he did, Chaiele."

"You have to be *Tateh*. The teeth of a fish even engraved the Yiddish *t* of *tateh* on your hand."

We went off arm in arm, she pulling me a little and I a little tipsy from the festival, from her, from the game between us that was going full sail. Her hand clutched mine where the moray had sunk its teeth. I felt tired and was afraid I was coming down with a fever that could rob me of the strength to get to the fire. I even saw one of the Germans who had been at the pizzeria but he wasn't at all aware of us, and I felt the cork for the demijohn in my pocket, and no, I was not tired. Caia was leaning heavily on my arm, shifting her weight onto me so that she was light, and she moved her feet as though she were dancing, or marching, making me list to one side. And I took on her weight and shuffled along at her festival, those last hours before her departure, before losing sight of her forever. I suddenly had the impulse to pick her up and lift her onto my shoulders. From a merry-go-round came the refrain of a popular song: "I'll never forget you, lovely Piedmontese girl, you'll be the only star that shines for me." And I was able to pick her up because she had become light and I heavy.

ℯℯℯ

No one took notice of me the whole time I was in the crowd. A few people said hello to Caia. The mob was pressing and at times we came to a complete halt. That was when she took the opportunity to kiss me on the cheek; my skin puckered where she had placed her lips. I returned her kiss, placing mine on her hairline at the top of her forehead, and under my palms I felt the beat of her life pulsing in her temples. "*Nu, nu,*" the pulses of your blood beat under my hands, in this mob I am yours, but so much yours, Chaiele, that I will never be able to belong to anyone else."

"You, mine," she told me, and pulled me, saying, "Come!" because something attracted her elsewhere.

Near the merry-go-round Daniele was talking to two foreign girls and making them laugh. Caia had confetti all over her and had become a little girl. As for me, my head was spinning with thoughts like, I've waited so long, Chaiele, to take you to a festival, to wander around the stands, to hold you close. It seems to me that I've been yours since the beginning of time, nor is this our first time. Is that how it is for you too, to become aware at the apex of happiness that there was a before and that this is a repetition? But I didn't say any of this, not wishing to disturb her childlike state, and wishing rather to follow her to her final pirouette of gaiety, until she fell into my arms fast asleep.

eee

We were approaching the open stretch of the pier and the jetty of the isthmus that leads to the castle. A band was playing on a platform. On a pedestal stood the figure of a female saint. Pinned to her robe were bank notes and slips of paper with writing on them. Caia led me to the plaster saint covered with strips of paper as she was covered with confetti and said, looking at her, "Don't I resemble her, *Tateh?*"

"The way life resembles a mannequin. You are alive, Chaiele, you are alive in the midst of a festival, and this store dummy is a poor imitation of your beauty. You are alive, Chaiele, and for one evening so am I, close to your life."

It was a solemn, resonant voice that came from a wooden throat, as from a guitar case. Even if I cleared my throat, it didn't bring back my own voice.

"Yes, yes, *Tatehle*, I am alive, that's why my name is Chaie, because it means life. It was you who gave it to me."

I read the lines written on the white slips pinned to the statue's robe. They were thanks for blessings received. One slip contained a line from the Bible: "Thus let all thine enemies perish, O Lord, but let those who love Him be as the rising sun in its might," Judges, Deborah. All your enemies will perïsh, my Chaiele, they will perish in this way, I thought, touching the cork in my pocket. She also read the slip and asked me in a little girl's voice, "And will you always love me?" distracting me from my thoughts about the fire and making me reply, "Like the rising sun in its might." And she laughed again with her chipped tooth. I closed my eyes, overcome with fatigue, and leaned against her.

"Good-bye, *Tateh.*"

When I heard her voice taking leave of me I roused myself and turned around, but Caia was still there holding my arm. Behind the statue I managed to get the frog out of my throat. My adolescent voice returned and my fatigue passed. I felt restored to myself, a relief mixed with emptiness. I was a boy again, light in years, once again uneasy about being with Caia, a name that means life, and until a moment ago I had known that, but at that moment I was surprised by it. I was surprised by everything. She had detached herself from her weight on my arm, from her childhood astride my shoulders. Caia was once again grown up, and the gratitude she had expressed earlier was now far away. The void on my arm informed me that I was once again myself.

We joined the others, who were already at the foot of the pier. They were eating watermelon and spitting the seeds at their feet. Daniele introduced the two German girls, who seemed nice and spoke a funny kind of English. Caia was very nice to them, speaking German and serving as interpreter for the rest of the evening. It was fascinating to watch her move from one language to the other, switching the sentences as they arrived and departed. I told her she was like a stationmaster and I would have liked to give her a whistle. She replied that trains had been her passion as a child and that she had made her father laugh when she told him she wanted to run a train. "Now you make languages travel," I said.

"Yes, those of others." A little naked doll peeked out of her pocket.

Daniele had his eye on one of the German girls and proposed going to see a movie at the open-air theater in the pine grove. On the island there were no closed movie theaters. It was unusual to opt for a movie, since there was always something better to do, but Daniele didn't want to end the summer with yet another serenade on the beach. Caia was a remarkable interpreter. Her German was a birdsong. In her mouth it melted into crisp syllables where consonants collided. It became a language that could joke and warble. Caia's voice managed to cleanse it in my ears. She knew how to handle wounds.

Daniele turned into a tour guide and showed the island to the two guests: stray dogs, oleanders, solemn turds left by the horses that drew the carriages, the bar that had the best gelati, pignoli to crack open and offer on the palm of the hand, taken by the fingers of the foreign girl who slowly selected the tiny nut from the center of the hand, thereby prolonging the contact for another second. The festival vanished in a buzz at our backs, and all together the group walked back up the road to the pine grove, untroubled by the impending good-byes. Daniele was a master at gags. Bursts of laughter rained down from the sky along with the flaming ribbons of the last clustered stars. The tallest pines left only a stripe of sky high up. We walked in the middle of the road to stay out in the open.

ccc

We came to the arena, as the opening between the trees was called, with its rows of folding wooden chairs and a screen that rippled in the wind, making waves on the faces of the actors. They were showing *For Whom the Bell Tolls.* Daniele sat next to his favorite.

I did not find a seat next to Caia but in the row behind her. She turned around, gesturing for me to put
my arms across the back of her seat. I did so and she
laid her head on them and I watched the film in the
most uncomfortable and most delicious position of
my entire life. The smell of her hair heavy with the
festive crowd and the noise, my fingers sticky with
pine resin, the sky stretched out above, descending
to the ground in a puff of warm breeze: it was air and
scent to breathe in and never again exhale. I inhaled
it, blocking out all other senses. I remember little
of the film, the breathless beauty of a wartime love.

Caia was leaning on my arms and I was so close
to her that her hair was just inches from my eyes.
For a while she would watch the film, then look up
at the night that roofed the movie house. She would
turn away from the story by leaning her head back
slightly, bringing it closer to mine. I would then
press my forehead against it and while she opened
her eyes wide to the darkness of the sky, I would
close mine in the back of her neck. I listened to the
beat of the pulse in my wrist which was holding up
her head. I felt the emptiness around us. We were
a tight cluster of grapes about to be picked. The
cluster trembles at the arrival of the harvesters, the
stem vibrates with pain at the sound of the nearby

scythes, but not us; we were steadfast and ready for the hand that would pluck us from that summer to make of us the fruit of a harvest.

At the end of the film, when Daniele's German girlfriend began to cry and someone else reached for a handkerchief and blew her nose, I wanted to say that there was nothing to cry about, that the two people in the story had shared a love, and that tears were a mistake because it was right, it was right like that. Caia rose up from the chair and my arms felt bare, but also free to move, no longer bound by the duty to serve as her support. The group broke up in last farewells, yawns, wisecracks.

"You're a good cushion."

"And you're a rascal."

Seeing him head toward the beach arm in arm with the German girl, someone called out, "Daniele, don't you know you live on the other side?" Before taking leave of the summer crowd, I managed to say without lowering my voice, "Good night, Chaiele."

I was alone. In my numbed arms a repressed strength was building up. My stomach muscles were so hard I could count them under my fingers. I was ready.

That night I sucked gasoline through the rubber hose from the tank of my father's car, filling the demijohn with five liters. I stoppered it with the cork and hid it. I did not go to the pensione for a final inspection, so as not to risk Daniele's return to our room before me. It was Caia's last night on the island. We had left each other with an appointment for the next day. I would carry her suitcase to the pier and we would walk together one more time.

ecc

Daniele came home late, completely disheveled. He had scored with the German girl and wanted to talk.

"Funny, one night you get into a fight with Germans and the next you make love with a German girl who's bright and amusing. What bizarre people."

"It could be that the children are better than the parents," I replied. "But look at you, you look as though you got into a worse fight tonight. That girl avenged her compatriots."

"You're right, it was a terrible vengeance, I can hardly stand up and my neck is full of bites. I couldn't help laughing at the memory of the night before. I tried to tell her that we got into a fight with Nazis. Hearing that word, she made a face of disgust and said *Scheisse*, meaning shit, Caia explained to me. A propos, you disappeared in the middle of the festival. I thought the two of you had gone off to say good-bye."

His familiarity suddenly struck me as inappropriate.

"No, we were surrounded by the crowd and we walked around the stands. But what about you?" I asked, to get Caia out of the conversation. "How did you meet the two girls?"

I didn't want anyone to talk about Caia again. I would have erased her from everybody's mind to keep her apart from the jumbled memories of a summer. I wanted to be the sole custodian of her name.

"It was easy, they couldn't make themselves understood by a vendor about the price of a brush. I intervened as interpreter. He was ripping them off. Then I offered them a slice of watermelon and finally you arrived with Caia and we had an official interpreter."

Once again a drop of acid rose in my throat at the sound of her name. I would have liked to correct him and tell him that her name was Chaie—Chaiele for me—and that even he, Daniele, had come close to her without knowing her. I went back to my diversionary tactic: "They were all alone, there wasn't anybody with them?"

"Completely alone. They arrived just in time for the festival. They come from Cologne, a city still in ruins, much worse than ours. It seems that after the war the only things still surviving were the cathedral and the Rhine. They grew up playing hide and seek in the rubble. They're fun. Marion was wild for kisses. Pity I'm leaving tomorrow."

ᴄᴄᴄ

Yes, leave, travel with Caia, take her to the train, in safety. What will happen here won't be able to touch her. She will be far away, she will be sleeping when a boy descends from his house at night to set a fire. It will be a fire far from her, from the losses she suffered, it will be a fire that won't compensate her, won't remove a single thorn. It's her father's fire. Chaiele, you wanted me to be like this, you gave me another name, you brought about unknown gestures in my body and a blood bond with you. I entrust you to Daniele; he will take you to safety before the fire.

Thoughts, decisive thoughts, were taking root in the center of my brain while I sat on the bed not listening to the end of that older boy's account of his evening. Good night. I grew up in the wake of your suffering, but before knowing you I spent a year asking books in what century I was living, and on what ground I trod. Meeting you was like the sun splitting my skin and the rough rocks hardening the soles of my feet. You made another skin grow over mine. You gave me access to the world by calling me yours. When you have left I will show what I'm capable of with my fire. It's not mine, I inherited it. I inherited your mourning along with the action that another father did not take in his lifetime. I inherited his debt, a fire in filial hands. You, Chaiele, called me *Tateh*. I accept it herewith. Tomorrow night I will be your *tateh* and I will burn your persecutors. It may be late to stop them, but it is only now that am I alive.

"Good night. Come on, let's go to sleep."

"Yes, Daniele, good night to you."

ϱϱϱ

Day came, and with it the sirocco that raised dust as high as the eyes. I left a note for Daniele, "See you at the port," but I couldn't get myself to write "with Caia." I was at her house early and was astonished that she was all ready to go. She said good-bye to her hosts, to the friend who had offered her that summer holiday on the island in exchange for her kindness at boarding school. She had left a beautiful gift for her. It was only then that I realized Caia must have means. I was the object of a few discreet witticisms about being her cavalier, but, like a good valet, I maintained my reserve. We left amid farewells and I expressed surprise over her single suitcase.

"I'm leaving everything here, I have no further use for summer clothes. I don't believe there will be another summer at the seashore. After this one it's not possible to wish for another." She spoke softly, making it hard to determine whether she was relieved or regretful. Because of the wind, she had tied a silk scarf around her hair and put on sunglasses. We walked past the beaches. The umbrellas were closed, few chairs were open, hardly any people.

The sea was beginning to swell. "It won't be an easy crossing," I said.

"Better that way. I'll think more about the sea and less about the land behind me. I came wanting to play at freedom. Now that I've finished secondary school, I'll go on to the university. I had a wonderful time here in this cordial, carefree south where a kiss lasts no time at all, less than diving into water. But it couldn't go on that smoothly. That's how you came along—gesturing like my father, discovering my background, my suffering as a child. You, a boy with your first trace of beard, covered with salt and the smell of fish, what the devil do you have to do with my father? And yet he chose you in order to be close to me, lovingly, steadily. And during his visit I became a child again. You gave me this. Last night at the festival I was happy to be your daughter. It made up for all the missing years. In that holiday crowd I relived half of the life I lost without him. I don't know what I did to you, kid, and I don't want to know. You came to me as a gift and I called you mine because my father was there, in you and on you. I don't know what we did to you. We took hold of you as the only hand that could bring our hands together. We besieged you with our need to find each other one last time. I can't even offer to apologize because for me this was a blessing."

"Even if all this is true and I was no more than an unlikely means of encounter, I felt love, Chaie, vast love, a reaching out over time. I experienced the ages that await me before I attain the affection and tenderness of an adult for a little daughter. You and your father gave me a purpose in this world, me, a bewildered kid, muted by awkwardness. You called me *Tateh*, *Tatehle*, the name you loved most in this world. So what if I missed out on your kisses which lasted no longer than a dive? I was there to kiss your forehead, give you my arm, buy you cotton candy, carry your suitcase. Now I want you to leave, to forget, to settle safely in some part of the world. I won't ask for an address in order to write to you, I won't leave you mine. We end here. We will not see each other again. I have to finish my summer, the one that changed my features. Soon I will go back to my home, to the city, I will give up my studies and find some kind of job. During this summer you liberated me. I can see my life from a height now, precisely on this day when I am losing you and the sirocco is blocking out even the island right in front. I can see myself out there alone, in a crowd that won't be festive. I see myself there all alone. Words of revolt, more blinding than this wind, are taking shape.

"On this island I learned freedom from the closed life of the city, pitiful freedoms of a body finally out in the open. The two of you have implanted love in my flesh, and are tossing me into the world like a rolling ball. Within love there is also anger, the sudden movement of getting up from a chair, as you showed me yourself. You called me outside, Chaie. Only you could have done that, only you whose name is life."

The wind carried off my words. I don't know if she heard them, if she wanted to hear them. She took my free arm and held it close to her side. We walked slowly with the wind that came from the sea. My skinny body was not enough to shelter her.

"You really put nothing in this suitcase."

She, stopped for a moment, then, with a metallic ring, a silver wire in her throat, she finally said, "I think we're very brave not to cry."

You had already used up every drop. I was awaiting a fire in the depth of the night of your departure. Not even the sirocco, which makes eyes tear, could squeeze a drop out of us.

ece

We went unhurried toward the departure, our hips pressing close, our legs touching. She set the pace, my barefoot stride adjusting to her closed city shoes. I could have walked on and on, the island would not have been big enough for me, nor the day; time itself would not have been long enough. My blood pulsed to the cadence of her steps, my breath came with their beats. I brushed my head against her scarf.

"Are we in step like this?" she asked.

"Very much so, as though our hearts were directing our feet. We form a single unit all the way to the port."

The U of the port appeared behind a curve and I told her that it was a volcanic lake dug by the Bourbons to the sea, that the island bubbled underneath with magma, that it healed sicknesses, leaving the body grateful. Sighting the boat, the words of a tour guide began tumbling out of my mouth, along with recommendations for preventing seasickness. I stopped babbling only when Daniele startled us from behind.

"From the back you look like a soldier with four legs, side by side in parade formation."

Taken by surprise, we stopped, smiling as we faced him, and he jokingly added, "At ease." Then we moved apart, breaking the minimal rank of two.

I went to buy the tickets. When I came back, Caia took off her glasses and untied her scarf. Her eyes were red but dry like mine. She took my hands and placed them at her temples.

"When I left my father the last time, at a train, I was afraid. I'm afraid now too, but for you."

I placed a kiss on her forehead, my hands burning with energy.

"Ciao, Tateh."

"Addio, Chaiele."

"*Ciao*, kid."

"*Ciao*, life. Don't worry about me, I'll be following the path you set me on."

Her eyes fell on my bony feet, sticking out of my jeans, and the trace of a smile appeared in her breath. She put the glasses and the scarf back on and turned toward the boat.

Daniele turned around, shook my hand like a good friend, took Caia's suitcase, and went up to her. She started moving toward the gangplank without looking back. I stayed there until the stern disappeared beyond the lighthouse, behind the pines. My hands were hot with power and I felt a violent impulse to move, to act. The sirocco was gaining force. Generally, it wrapped me in indolence; this time, it unleashed a tarantella in my blood. I turned my back to the port and the wind grabbed me by the shoulders, pushing me forward, and in its hot breath I began to run. Caia was no longer on one arm and her suitcase on the other. I was light, restraining the soles of my feet so as not to lengthen my stride too much. I was running uphill. I hadn't run for some time and I was astounded by how agile, how fast I was.

I stopped at home to make sure my things were ready. Then I joined Nicola at the beach. He had not gone out to sea.

"It lasts three days, this wind. All we can do is put out some traps in the bay and hope for octopus."

I picked up one of the traps and looked at it without saying much. In every trap for fish there is a way our, but the fish don't find it. Looking at that simple device, I felt like a fish, incapable of figuring it out.

I looked at the heaving sea. I saw Caia's ferry, which had not attempted to enter the Procida channel because it was too rough and had made a detour farther out, passing in front of the fishermen's beach. I saw the prow pitching and rolling. Caia was surely remembering to hold on tight and keep her eyes focused straight ahead so as not to vomit, as I had suggested. Daniele was there to help her.

"Daniele is on that ferry returning to the city," I pointed out to Nicola.

"Better today, tomorrow will be worse," he replied.

The boat was beached. I touched it with my palm. The wood was smooth from the salt and the yearly painting, and the oars had carved a groove near the stem of the oarlock at the point of friction. The tiller of the rudder was dark where the hand held it. Every piece showed wear, handling, softening, rounding from use. I slid my hand along the rim of the bow.

"Do you polish the boat?" I asked with a feeling of tenderness.

"As you can see, the wood has its grain. When we cut it to make planks we always respect that. If it's cut against the grain, the wood warps, it rebels, and so much so that in the end it splits. Even seasoned wood is like that, it's worked with the grain. A boat is polished along the direction of the wood's grain. It's rubbed from bow to stern, the way the sea does it."

"I'm stroking it because the season is over. I won't be coming fishing anymore."

The wind rose from the sea, coming from Capri and hitting our shore of the island with force.

"How do you feel about the sirocco?" I asked.

"It's the worst wind. It changes the face of the island. It blows away a beach on one side and carries it over to the other. The sirocco is not a wind, it's a fury. The sky disappears, hot air hits the head, preventing it from reasoning. One should not conceive children when the sirocco blows, or make decisions. It ignites fires. It makes the bell ring, do you hear it?"

A dour peal rose on the current of the wind and weakly reached the beach. "It's a furious wind."

Caia's ferry had turned the island's cape and could no longer be seen.

I said good-bye to Nicola and went to Uncle's house. I saw him at the gate, speaking with a woman in his little garden.

"Just wanted to thank you for all the times you let me go fishing this summer."

He acknowledged my thanks with a nod and gave me a smile I had never before received from him. It was brief, intimate, then, the smile gone, he nodded again. It was his "yes" to me, a rare masculine "yes" that took note of me for the first time. I was not so dim-witted as to let this go to my head. For the first time he was accepting this nephew who carried his name. In that moment we coincided in a name, but that night I would have another, which I could not share.

At home, my father was at the dinner table. Already then there was talk about things to be done for our return to the city. The sirocco determined the end of the summer. He looked at me attentively and well disposed.

"I'm not sorry that the return to the city will scrape off some of that wild crust, but I am sorry to see you get back into a pair of shoes. Your bare feet put me in a good mood."

In reply to his good humor I joked, "I put on shoes every year the way a convict attaches the chain to his feet. The first days I can barely walk. At least once I'd like to try and wear sandals right through the winter, like Franciscans."

"It seems to me that for the past year it's not just the sandals of monks that interest you. Are you perhaps becoming a believer?"

"No, all I became this summer is more of a fisherman," I said, trying to keep our conversation in check, because we had moved from shoes to faith in too much of a hurry.

"I knew that you were seeing Daniele's older friends, and that you had a crush on one of the girls."

I was grateful to him for not pronouncing her name, and responded in a subdued voice, "I didn't get anywhere. Uncle was right to tell me to find a more suitable girl."

It was strange for us to be talking about such things. I tried to find the most ordinary words.

"Were you very disappointed?" he asked.

"Only a little."

He looked at me searchingly. "Something is happening to you. You've acquired a terseness, a precision. You no longer accompany your words with your hands. You also stand straighter. It has done you good to be with older boys. Except that I'm a little worried about this sudden change. A father is prepared for his son to grow taller, catch up with him, surpass him, but he finds it hard to follow the transformations of his character. Yours I don't yet know how to define, you don't resemble anyone in our family. Can you help me out?"

He was being sincere. He found himself faced with a hardened son and was trying to understand him. I didn't want to betray myself, say something that might be remembered the day after the fire. Nor did I want to repulse that rare intimacy.

"For the past year I see only wrongs. I acknowledge the debts that have come down to me. Last year you and Mama had to sign a document renouncing Grandpa's estate because of debts. I discovered this year that I can't do what you did. I see our city held in the grip of people who have sold it to the American army. I see foreign soldiers drunkenly pissing in our streets, I see women clinging to their trousers. These things have been around for some time, but I'm just discovering them now. I see that they don't matter to anybody, nobody is offended, nobody is ashamed. I see that the war has humiliated us. Elsewhere it was over a long time ago, for us it goes on. I don't know how to answer your question, I don't know how to answer anything. However, the spring to answer is winding up inside of me."

He listened to me, frowning. My remarks prompted him to defend himself, to take the other side. From there it was easy to go back to the recent past, to the war. For once he did not try to get out of it. He started to talk again in order to understand, not because he had already understood.

"You're right to learn about the recent past; it is your right and also something that doesn't interest most of your contemporaries. But I have the impression that you're not going about it in a reasonable way. This may sound strange, but it seems to me that you want to enter into the past in order to correct it. You criticize it with an eye to changing it, but that can't be done. Not even God can do anything about that. It's already quite a lot to protect the present from mistakes, from causing harm that has to be repaired. That's a lot even if it's not enough, for to have done no harm does not save one from guilt. In difficult times which you didn't know—and it's not said that you need to experience them—in difficult times, to have done no harm is to become an accomplice of harm."

He was looking beyond me and stopped, displeased by what he had said. "Accomplice is an inaccurate term and is also unfair," he started up again, talking directly to me, holding me responsible for the word that he was refuting. "I didn't know how to stand up to harm. I knew later, but even now I can't be sure I would have acted appropriately. I lived in Rome. I knew that in Via Tasso they were torturing partisans. I never came near that street. I was one of the many, not one of the few, but an accomplice, no. If you wish to become one of the few, direct your attention to the present. Leave the past alone. You weren't there, it is not your responsibility."

He knew nothing about Caia, but I felt I had been exposed by him. And then what? Even if he had read my face and it was not just a flash of intuition, I would not have changed my mind. I didn't want to deny or ever admit, and so I remained imprisoned in silence, awkwardly staring at my feet. Then he ended his speech.

"It's wrong of me to talk to you this way. You're still a boy with a wide margin for growth and I'm already attributing definitive things to you. In the meantime, your answer will be study, school, and respect. Can I count on that?"

He was once again the father of a young boy and he received the reply of a mechanical yes in conclusion. The thrust of his intuition had retreated and I shrugged off the intrusion of his intelligence.

ecc

I wandered through the streets. Pine needles and pinecones lay scattered by the wind. Now, my footsteps made a rustling sound and the needles tickled my feet. I had to remember that for the night. Should I remain barefoot or put on shoes? I decided barefoot was better. I walked past the pensione; the car was not there.

I carefully examined the little gate operated by a latch. There were no dogs; on the island no one had guard dogs. There were no trees that could catch fire. The wind would have spread a fire. My thoughts raced ahead and set up hypotheses. I weighed them and rejected them. I was focused on only one thing, aimed at a target.

I ambled around the island to relieve a pressure of readiness that did not want to wait. I had nothing else to do, no fishing, no beach. I walked over to the meeting place of the younger crowd. Eliana was there with a girlfriend. She greeted me warmly, then left her friend and came over to me.

"I'm glad you're still here. When are you leaving?"

"When the sirocco stops."

She too had her hair under a scarf. She had not come in search of me. She looked at me trustingly, opening herself up to the risk of being hurt. Was I still unresponsive? In order not to embarrass her I lowered my eyes.

"When this wind stops I'll come to see you. I'll have shoes on my feet and hair washed in fresh water. I'll come to see you in the city. Nicola told me no one should make plans when the sirocco blows."

I told her this in order to believe in a future, beyond that night, even if I couldn't see myself beyond the fire. That was where the boundary was drawn. What do animals think, unaware of a future, focused on the brief renewal of the day? Is that how prisoners think? The wind forced us to cling to a wall.

"No plans. But is this a promise? If it is, then I want to wait for the end of the sirocco."

I smiled and looked at her at last. The search for happiness was written all over her face. I gave a quick nod of agreement, then I said it, a firm, serious yes. And she leaned forward for a kiss. I turned my cheek slightly but she came squarely at my mouth, rapid, direct, like her words. The thought came to me that a person as frank as she also gave real kisses, kisses that would not settle for a cheek.

"Thanks," I said.

"What for?" she asked, already heading back to her girlfriend.

"For the lip balm."

She turned back to smile, holding on to the scarf on her head with one hand.

eee

I walked for hours. There was no one around; the wind had depopulated the island. No one wanted to be outside. I made an inspection of my sites. I didn't look beyond the night to come, beyond the fire. I didn't ask myself if I would get away with it, if I would avoid burning myself, being discovered, getting caught. At the time, I didn't even know that there was a prison for juveniles. I didn't want to know. I had to get as far as the fire. The aftermath might amount to nothing. I no longer had a home, a family, a future, all I had was an urgent present. I was alone in the world in that fire. The sirocco had no rest; neither did I. I felt good in that wind, it sharpened my senses, it brought the heat to my nostrils, and to my ears the noise of windows and doors rattling. It wiped out tracks, muffled sounds, hid the stars.

There was no sunset. As though extinguished, the light went out, night fell. I went back to the pensione and found the car there. At home they had left my dinner on the fully set table. I went outside to eat. I chewed slowly, as I like to do, eating unhurriedly. Then I felt sleepy. I had to wait for the middle of the night, but I'd never make it if I tried to stay awake. I went to my room and lay down on the floor. The absence of comfort would ensure that my sleep was brief. I found a position on my side and fell asleep. I awoke twice, the second time when my parents came home. I jumped into bed. My mother opened the door to see if I was there. I heard them go into the bathroom, exchange a few words, turn out the light. They fell asleep quickly. I waited, my eyes on the ceiling. The wind pushed the island out to sea; it was a raft adrift, way off course, losing the survivors of a shipwreck.

I got up and opened the window. I had been mistaken in my calculations: I could not lower myself from there, leaving the window open to rattle and make noise. I would have to leave by the front door without making a sound. It took endless minutes to turn the knob, reach the entrance, get outside.

Barefoot, I felt the wind come at me, billowing my clothes. It took me by the throat but was not hostile; it was a dog that wagged its tail and whimpered loudly. I took the matches, the newspaper, and the demijohn of gasoline. The streets were paths of dust, debris rolling along as though carried by a current. A hunting dog came up to me and walked beside me for a good bit of the way. At the corner of the pensione he left me.

All along the way I had the wind on all sides, but in the last street it hit me head on, in the face. The night of the storm came back: *"Né paù,"* don't be afraid, Nicola's voice at my back and the crash of the sea. *"Né paù,"* I gestured with my head, I'm not afraid. There was not a light. I squeezed my eyes shut against the dust and forged ahead from memory. I had decided to do without a flashlight, trusting myself. I felt the car, the gate, raised the latch, and was inside. I kept the gate open with a stone so that it wouldn't slam shut. Just a few meters to reach the door at the top of a few stairs. Next to the railing there was a covered corner. I huddled over to try out a match: it didn't go out.

Don't watch me, Chaiele, sleep in your train, forget the island, the summer.

I opened the demijohn and poured the gasoline on the door, slowly, so as not to splash any on my feet. I didn't pour all of it, keeping the rest to slosh on the car. I moved in the dark with precise gestures, and could see better than before. I thought of nothing. I did what I had to do and that's all, and I knew how to do it and it seemed obvious to me that I would know how. In the covered corner I lit a match and a sheet of newspaper. I held it to the door. Not at once, but after a few seconds the gasoline reacted with explosive force and I fell, thrown backward. I had been wise not to use the whole newspaper. The pages used as a wick had been torn from my hand by the fire. Now the fire blazed along the door and shattered the pane of glass set into it. I straightened up, blinded, clutching the remaining sheets. I lit them and left the walkway to set fire to the car as well. Before it took, I heard the shouts, *Feuer, Feuer,* and finally the car also burst into flame. I threw the demijohn at it. The savagery of my gestures kept me calm. In the street, the fire had become bright as day, the noise louder than the wind, and the heat ferocious:

Windows were flung open. Behind me, voices, shrieks. I was already in the middle of the street, running with the wind at my back, fast, light, the darkness cloaking my shoulders and a dog at the corner of the street waiting to run beside me. Behind me a fire erupted that could not change the past.

about the author

ERRI DE LUCA was born in Naples in 1950 and today lives in the countryside near Rome. He is the author of several novels, including *God's Mountain*, *Three Horses* (Other Press), and *The Day Before Happiness* (Other Press). He taught himself Hebrew and translated several books of the Old Testament into Italian. He is the most widely read Italian author alive today.